ROSES WHERE THORNS GROW

KARI H. SAYERS

ISBN: 978-1-68046-834-2

Published by Satin Romance
An Imprint of Melange Books, LLC
White Bear Lake, MN 55110
www.satinromance.com

Published in the United States of America.

Cover Design by Ashley Redbird Designs

ACKNOWLEDGMENTS

I wish to thank colleagues and friends who have encouraged me, made suggestions, and checked facts during the process of writing this novel. I would especially like to thank Dr. Montague Blundon III, MD, Joan Cashion, Dr. Duncan Earle, Dana Graham, Sharon Johnson, Antoinette and John Lane, Dr. Greg Levonian, Matthew Nadelson, Bruce Schwartz, and Dr. Charles Spurgeon.

CHAPTER ONE

FIRST MEETING

The cabin sits on a bluff, a mile above a popular resort town in the San Bernardino Mountains. It is surrounded by tall sugar pines, majestic black oaks, a lone dogwood tree, and lots of red cedars. The steep slope in front is covered by purple-flowered Vinca, while the rest of the grounds are kept *au naturel* with tufts of grass, little cedar saplings, and weeds of various kinds. The only sounds come from the pecking of woodpeckers, the squawking of blue jays, and an occasional distant din from cars driving into the resort.

The deck on the second level of the small cabin overlooks the driveway below and the sparkling blue lake in the distance. I spend most of my time on this level because that's where the kitchen, living room, master bedroom, and bathroom are. Upstairs, there are more bedrooms and another bathroom, and downstairs there is a mud room and what the local realtors call a great room with a billiard table and a second television set.

I had come up to the mountains to do some troublesome writing. I needed the fresh mountain air to clear my mind and finish my latest novel, so as soon as the finals were over, the grades turned in, and the requisite reports written, I drove up from my home in the Los Angeles area. It was the end of May, and because I hadn't been up here much after my husband Robert died, spider webs were everywhere. I immediately called Rose and her crew to come and give the place a thorough cleaning, and after I had swept the leaves and other debris from the driveway, I decided to walk down to see my artist friend Cindy and her husband Chad to thank them for keeping an eye on my property while I was away.

It was only a five-minute walk downhill along a narrow, winding road. The only cars I saw were a couple of construction trucks that passed me and turned left where the road forks. I took the other path. The few cabins on both sides of me stood there silently shuttered up and expressionless, waiting for vacationers. Cindy's house sat on a large corner lot, tastefully landscaped with Japanese maples, rhododendrons, and even roses like an oasis among the many native pines all around. Her little red sports car was parked outside.

Cindy was home and came to the door. Her black hair hung like a curtain down both sides of her freckled face. She smiled and smoothed down a kind of purple smock that she was wearing before giving me a hug and motioning me to come inside to look at her latest paintings. Frameless canvases of landscapes in subdued colors were propped up against the big stone fireplace and on easels around the living room that served as her studio.

"They're good," I said. "You're truly talented."

"Thank you," she said. "I hope to have a small exhibition at the resort later this summer. And I want you to come."

"I'd love to come," I replied.

She looked at me. "How long is it since Robert passed away now?" she asked me after a while.

"About two years. Why?"

"Are you seeing anyone yet?"

"No, not really."

"Are you interested?"

"Maybe one of these days. Do you have someone in mind for me?"

"I may have. He's quite a catch really, although there are issues."

I walked back to my place at a happy clip. The crisp spring air made my face tingle, and I didn't give Cindy's comments another thought.

On Sunday morning I finally sat down at the computer to write. I was working on my fifth mystery novel and was writing profiles of the cadre of suspects I had rounded up. The murder scene was complete. My sleuth Jule McCormick had found the victim, a Chinese-American pianist and voice coach by the name of Larry Wong, in a pool of blood on the floor of his condo in the Bunker Hill Towers in downtown LA. She had returned there the morning after a party that Larry had hosted for his students and friends to retrieve her cell phone and had immediately called the police and offered her assistance. It was not the first time she had helped the LAPD solve a case. The guests at the party were the primary suspects, but I had trouble making them come to life.

Around noon I made myself a cup of coffee and walked out on the deck. As I looked over the railing, I saw a man in a tight, white tee-shirt, khaki pants, and high-top hiking boots bending over one of the sprinklers. I set my coffee down on the patio table and called down to him, "Hi! Can I help you?"

He stood up and called back, "A couple of your sprinkler heads are leaking. We have a serious drought up here, and if the water police see it, they'll fine you big time." He paused before he continued, "I can fix it for you. I'm a licensed contractor, and that's my truck down there."

A white truck with a logo that said Construction Company and a name I couldn't read was parked at the bottom of the driveway. I noticed fleetingly that he was a handsome man about my age, built like a contractor, muscular and tanned with dark brown hair combed back but with unruly strands falling down over his temples on both sides in the style of an English school boy. "How much do you charge?" I asked.

"Ten dollars and a cup of coffee," he called back.

"That sounds like a good deal," I said. "Go ahead."

"Okay, I'll get a screwdriver and a pair of pliers from my truck and have it fixed in five minutes."

He started walking down toward his truck. I came down to meet him, and I read Cronin Construction Company in big letters on the truck door.

"I'm Chris," he said as he came back up the driveway with his tools in one hand and a newspaper in the other.

"Megan," I said and held out my hand.

He put the newspaper on the retaining wall in front of the cabin. "Nice to meet you. Megan Viets, right? I have seen you on your power-walks around the area, and your friend Cindy down the road told me that you live alone up here. Aren't you afraid living here by yourself?"

Oh, so this was the guy Cindy had in mind for me. Interesting!

"No, should I be?" I said.

"Well, we sure have our share of crime around here. If you read the local paper, it sounds like we're the crime capital of the world, but as long as you keep your doors locked, you should be all right."

He went about working on the sprinklers, and I went upstairs to the kitchen to make coffee.

"Do you like your coffee with milk and sugar," I called down from the deck while the single-cup coffee maker did its work.

"No, just black, thank you."

I made two cups and took them down with my ten-dollar bill.

The sprinklers were soon fixed, and we sat down on the retaining wall with our coffee, and I gave him the ten dollars.

"Good coffee," he said.

"Thank you. It's Starbucks."

"Cindy told me you're a writer," he continued. "And you actually publish what you write. Several novels, right?"

"Yes, have you read any of them? I write mystery novels, and I've come up here to finish my fifth one."

"I'm sorry. I haven't read any of them yet, but I will." He paused. "I understand you're giving a workshop at the high school for our so-called Mountain Writers on Thursday."

"You're well informed," I said

"It's a small town. Everyone knows everything about everybody's business around here. And it's also been in the newspaper."

"Really?"

"Yeah, the *Mountain Gazette* ran an article about it this week. I brought you a copy. It has your picture in it too." He pointed to the newspaper.

"Thank you. That's very sweet of you," I said.

"I'm planning to be there by the way."

"Oh, a contractor who's also a writer, I see."

He smiled showing a straight row of white teeth like a string of pearls. "Not exactly. I've been deputized to be a security guard for the event."

"Really? Or are you pulling my leg?"

"Well, not exactly. My brother is the sheriff, and there's a lot of drug dealing going on around the schools. I know this place looks like an idyllic little paradise, but that's just a cover. Underneath there's a lot of dry rot. More than a dozen students at the high school overdosed on heroin and died last year alone. We have a heroin epidemic on our hands."

"More than twelve teenage school children overdosed on heroin? That's incredible."

"We nab one dealer, and another one steps right up to take his place. That's why all events at the high school have security on hand. And that's why I'm telling you to lock your doors. I'll give you my cell phone number in case you see something or have trouble." He set down his cup and took out a card. "And here's the sheriff's private cell phone number in case you can't reach me or get through to 9-1-1." He took a pen from his pocket and wrote down an additional number on his card.

"I'd never call the sheriff's private number."

"It's okay in an emergency."

His penetrating gaze unnerved me a little, and I turned away. As he finished his coffee, he turned around and looked at my miserable shed.

"I see you need a new shed door," he said. "I'll take a look at it if you want."

We both walked over to the shed that also needed some new paint. "How much will a new door cost me?" I asked.

"A couple of hundred bucks. And it should open from the other side, right?"

"Yes, that would be easier."

"And we could build a couple of steps in front to make it easier to go in and out."

"That would be nice too."

"I'll send a couple of guys over tomorrow to look at it."

We walked around the cabin together. The ground was soft, the stately oaks sported fresh green leaves, and my dogwood tree showed off a profusion of frothy white blossoms.

"The roof looks good," he said. "It's a good, solid little cabin."

"That's good to hear." It wasn't a bad idea to make friends with a handyman. Robert had been handy, and although he had been enthusiastic about the cabin the first year after we bought it, he had been so occupied with his work that he hadn't wanted to come up all that often in the end.

"You're still wearing a wedding band, I see. But you're not married, are you?"

"No, my husband died almost two years ago."

"Oh, I'm sorry."

"It's okay."

"What happened?"

"He died in a plane crash in North Africa. He was one of those crazy bush pilots, flying people and cargo and who knows what all over the place. We were married for eight years."

"Children?"

"No." I stopped and remained silent for a while. I wasn't ready to share my whole life story with this guy yet. "What about you?"

"I live alone with my dog and a housekeeper who comes in a few hours every day."

His tone was full of melancholy, and already I wondered how such a good-looking man could go uncalled for, although Cindy had hinted he had issues. I guessed he might be just a little older than I was.

"When's your birthday?" he asked suddenly.

"17th of September."

He didn't say anything but slowly took out his wallet and showed me his California driver's license. Height: 6'-01" and Weight: 180 lbs. Date of Birth: September 17, but a year before me. We both laughed at the strange coincidence.

"I should probably get back to my dog. I need to check on a couple of work sites too, to make sure everything is ready for the guys to start early tomorrow morning. Thank you again for the coffee."

"Don't you need a down payment or something before you start your work?"

"It's okay. I'll take a chance on you."

"Thanks."

"I'll check the timer for the sprinklers before I leave. I see that it's right by the front door." He took the stairs up to the door in two leaps and quickly adjusted the dials. Then he waved goodbye, and I just stood there looking after him as he walked down the driveway and drove away in his truck. I picked up the paper and checked that everything about the workshop was correct. The picture was an old one from the publisher. I was pleased to see my new book mentioned. Maybe it would mean more sales.

CHAPTER TWO

DINNER AT SETTLERS INN

The next day, two workmen showed up to measure and generally look at the shed, and I went out to talk to them about the direction of the door and the steps. "Where's Chris today?" I asked the one who seemed to be in charge.

"He's down the hill to bid on other jobs," he answered in fluent English but with a Spanish accent. "He'll probably come by tomorrow."

They both seemed capable people. "How do you like working for Chris?" I asked. I figured I'd do a little spying too.

"He's a good guy. He takes good care of us and pays more than some other contractors around here."

"He probably gets better people that way." I said. "What's your name?"

"Ben and this is Carlos."

"Hi, I'm Megan."

"We'll go and get the wood and angles and the other material we need," Ben said. "Then we'll come back and take the old door out."

I went inside and sat down at the computer, but I was too distracted to write anything, so I decided to go for a walk. On my way back, I passed by Cindy's house. She was on her way out, car keys in hand, but she stopped to chat.

"I understand you've talked about me to a contractor named Chris," I said. "Is he the guy you had in mind for me then?"

"Chris Cronin?"

"Yes, I guess that's his last name. He was driving a Cronin Construction Company truck."

"I'm so glad you two have gotten together. I had told him about you earlier, but I haven't talked to him since I saw you the other day."

"Well, we haven't exactly gotten together. He's doing some work for me, and that's all."

"Chris is a nice guy, but he's had a couple of rough years."

"What happened?"

"I'll let him tell you the way he wants to present it. Don't listen to all the gossip." She passed by me and got ready to step into her car. "Trust me. I would never have encouraged him to introduce himself to you if I hadn't felt absolutely sure that he's a good person through and through. Maybe it won't click between you, but at least he'll be a good friend and handy too. I've got to go. I have a doctor's appointment."

As if it wasn't enough that I was in the middle of my own mystery novel and had trouble with the suspects, now I had a real-life mystery on my hands.

Walking home, I tried to go over my novel in my head. I was contemplating adding the openly gay security guard in Larry's building as an additional suspect. My private detective had done some clever sleuthing in the meantime and learned that Larry was gay, which surprised everyone because he had never discouraged the female students, who clearly had a crush on him, from flirting with him. It furthermore gave me a chance to look differently at Ruth, the righteous Christian zealot, who was also Larry's voice student. A soprano in her church choir, she had buried two husbands under somewhat mysterious circumstances. It was no secret that she had fallen madly in love with the bushy-haired, tall, and talented Chinese-American musician. A bit off center, she could have tried to seduce Larry, and when he failed to respond, she could have confronted him and killed him in a fit of passionate rage. Then there was Larry's former roommate who had suddenly gone back to Indiana, where he was from, and the Chinese-American student who had grown up with Larry in Chinatown and had ties to the Chinese mafia. There was also an interesting drug dealer who lived downstairs from Larry. The story was beginning to take form.

When I came back to the cabin, the two men had removed the old shed door and placed a big piece of plywood against the opening, with other wooden planks spread out on the ground.

They returned the next day and started sawing and hammering, soon placing the new, custom-made door in place. Chris showed up later, and I went out to talk to him.

"How's everything going?" he asked.

"Good, I think. I hope they know what they're doing."

"They do, and the door is going to look great," he said, taking off his sunglasses and flashing his pearly white teeth at me again. His blue-green eyes seemed to glitter in the sunlight.

"Are you doing anything special tonight?" he asked.

"No, why?"

"Have you tried the food at Settlers Inn over on the highway?"

"No. Is this an invitation?"

"Yes, I'd like to take you there. It's really a great place. People come from all over and on the weekend, it's hard to get a table unless you make a reservation way in advance."

"That would be nice. Do you take all your clients to dinner?"

"No, only young, sporty widows who write books."

I was at a loss for a snappy answer.

"I'll call over there to see what's going on." He took out his cell phone and called. "Al, my man, I'm taking a client over to dinner. What's cookin' tonight?... Sounds good. We'll come early for drinks." He hung up. "How about I pick you up in an hour? I have a couple of jobs in the area that I need to check on and make sure they're closed up."

"Okay, I'll be ready."

It was a little over an hour before he returned, with a light sports coat slung over one shoulder. The men had packed up and left.

"Are you okay with walking over there?" he asked. "It's no more than half a mile. And remember to bring a jacket. It cools off at night up here as you know."

I went inside to grab a wrap, and we started our trek over to the highway. "How many jobs do you have around here?" I asked.

"The one down the road you've probably seen. There was a fire caused by a gas explosion, and the fire department flooded the place. It had to be completely gutted. The other new construction is close to the resort, and another big remodeling job is on the north side of the lake. Then there are some smaller jobs farther up the hill. Contractors around here have to make hay in the summer, you know."

"What do you do in the winter?"

"Some go on booze cruises to Mexico. I bid on jobs in the lowland. Right now, I'm the backup on a job for the Redlands School District. That's a big job."

"Do you stay down there then?"

"Yes, my father moved to San Bernardino when he retired from the business last year. He actually started the construction company by building or resurfacing federal highways for the government back in the seventies. There was a lot of money in that and still is, but we decided to get out."

"Why did you do that if it was such a good deal?"

"There's a lot of corruption—bidding high, the bids based on high wages for more workers than needed but then hiring illegal or undocumented workers for less than minimum wages. I don't want to deal with it any more, although it's hard to give up the money."

We had to step aside and walk single-file when several cars passed us on the narrow road. I walked behind him and couldn't help noticing how well built he was, a real specimen as my brother back in Wisconsin would say, with arms and shoulders that had done a lot of lifting and some heavy physical work. What kind of a rough life could a guy like this have had?

"How's your book coming?" he asked.

"It's coming along slowly."

"What's it about?"

"Well, it's actually based on a true murder case. Larry Wong, a tall, good-looking Chinese-American music teacher at a small college has been murdered, brutally stabbed to death in what looks like a crime of passion. My sleuth, Jule McCormick, a highly intelligent and slightly eccentric ex-nun turned psychology professor, finds him on the floor in a pool of blood the morning after a party at his condo when she goes back to retrieve her cell phone. She goes on to research the victim's life and help the somewhat clueless police detectives."

"And who dun it?"

"I'm not going to tell you." I smiled coyly. "I have a group of suspects, mostly guests at the party, and I'm now trying to write their biographies or profiles."

He stopped and pointed to a construction site among the trees. "See the construction going on down the hill? That's going to be a great new house for a retired lawyer."

"Nice location, I'm sure."

"Yes, prime."

The big neon sign that announced "Settlers Inn" came into view, and as we reached the front door, Chris put on his coat and ushered me in first. The restaurant had the ambiance of a mountain lodge with dark paneled walls and small, square-paned windows and even though it was a weekday, it was crowded. Robert and I had planned to have dinner here one night, but something had come up, and we never made it.

"Hello Mr. Cronin," the hostess greeted us. "I believe Al has a table ready for you. He's over there." She pointed over to the side.

Chris waved as the formally dressed Al approached us. "How's it going, my friend?" Chris greeted him. "Al, this is my new client Megan Viets. She's a writer. Megan, this is Al, the dude that owns this joint."

"Glad to meet you, Ma'am. Are you staying for the summer?"

"Yes, that's my plan."

"How do you like our mountain community so far?" he asked as he guided us over to a table by the window overlooking the lake.

"It's beautiful and peaceful compared to Los Angeles."

He held out my chair, and we sat down. "Drinks?" he asked Chris.

"Yes." Chris turned to me. "A glass of red wine?"

"Sounds good." Al left us and brought back two glasses of wine.

"So, you grew up here then I take it," I said to Chris.

"Yeah, my father came out here from Kansas City and built the business. I graduated from the high school we're going to on Thursday." He paused. "And then my father thought I should see some more of the world, just like my older brother, so I went to a university in New York to study engineering for a year but hated it. And so, I came back and worked in the business before finishing my business degree at Arizona State." He hesitated for a moment and took a sip of wine. "I was not a great student, but miraculously I managed to graduate after three years." He looked at me and smiled. "My father would only let me join the business if I started at the bottom, so I lived with the illegal day laborers in trailers out on the highways. I didn't mind it too much. I guess you could say it built character."

A waiter came to take our orders, and I let Chris decide as I had no idea what the specialty was here. It turned out to be the best lobster bisque I'd ever tasted, followed by filet mignon and more red wine.

"So, where'd you grow up?" Chris asked.

"On a dairy farm in Wisconsin. I came out to California to go to college at USC and did well in school, so I went on to graduate school at UCLA, where I met my husband, Robert." I paused to take a few spoonfuls of the bisque before I continued. "Robert was crazy about flying. He went to flight school and took lessons to get different ratings. After I graduated, we got married and moved to Dubai, where I got a job as a journalist for an English newspaper."

"That must have been exciting and a lot of fun. A long way from Wisconsin, though."

"Yes, that's for sure. Then we moved around to different places in North Africa. For a while we lived in Lagos, Nigeria, and we even spent a year in Saudi Arabia, where my husband worked as a corporate pilot for a wealthy businessman. But because of the unrest in the Middle East and North Africa, I came back to Los Angeles after five years. A couple of years earlier, we had bought a house here and also the cabin. Robert kept flying people and cargo all over Africa, although he came home quite often. Two years ago, his plane crashed in a severe sandstorm."

"While you were here in California?"

"Yes, it was a shock at first, but I've more or less gotten over it. Bringing the coffin home and preparing for the funeral all seems like a blur now. He had a good life insurance policy, but I'll have to sell the house. I plan to buy a condominium and, hopefully, keep the cabin."

"Are your parents still alive?"

"Yes, they still live on the farm in Wisconsin." I paused. "And you, you've talked about your father, but what about your mother?"

"She died of breast cancer when I was eight years old. My brother Ed was almost thirteen and helped take care of me, and we had a housekeeper, Maria, the same one who's now my housekeeper. My father retired a year ago and moved off the mountain as I mentioned."

We ate in silence for a while. I noticed that while Chris talked freely about the business and his parents, he did not mention anything about his private life or any relationships. There had obviously been some. After all, he was a personable guy with a seemingly successful business.

We finished off with coffee and got ready to start our trek back. It was pitch black outside. The lights from the city did not reach this altitude. It had cooled off, and I was glad I had brought my wrap. We walked along the narrow road that only allowed for single file the few times a car approached.

Chris showed great interest in astronomy and pointed out the various constellations—Orion's Belt, the Big Dipper, the North Star, the Milky Way, and others. "There's got be some life out there somewhere," he mused. "It doesn't make sense that we'd be the only living things in this enormous universe."

"I agree. The question, I think, is where. But our puny brains cannot understand this vast universe. The scientists at JPL are smart, and it must be exciting to do what they do, but it's difficult stuff."

It seemed like no time before we were walking up my driveway.

"Look at all the bats flying toward your cabin," he said as a colony of flying rats flew right over our heads at an amazing speed.

"They sure are ugly," I said and stopped to look at them more closely as they suddenly turned around in mass confusion. "So ugly that surely only a mother could love them."

He looked at me sternly. "All creatures have their place and are useful for something, the homely ones too. These remarkable flying mammals eat insects, pollinate flowers, eat fruit, and spread seeds." He hesitated and turned away to look after the disappearing flock.

His thoughtfulness and wisdom surprised me. I didn't expect such a handsome man to have this kind of knowledge and understanding of homely creatures. "Thank you for a wonderful meal," I said after a few moments. "The food was really good—and the company too."

"I'll walk you up the stairs to the door to see that you get in and that all is safe."

"Okay."

At the door, he stroked my face lightly to brush back some uncooperative strands of hair, and his touch made my pulse beat faster and sent an electric current through my body.

"I'll see you at the high school the day after tomorrow," he said.

Then he leaped down the stairs, jumped into his truck, and drove off.

I walked into the dark cabin and had to admit to myself that I felt a little lonely. But it would not have been appropriate to invite him in. He might have gotten the wrong idea. And he wasn't even my type. As the French would say, *Tout dans les bras, rien dans la tête.* (All in the arms, nothing in the head.) But that was a silly cliché and a stereotype. Just because someone was good-looking, didn't mean he couldn't be smart too. After all, this guy knew how to run a business, manage people, and sell his services. "What could the gossip be about?" I wondered. I had to find a way to get him to talk.

CHAPTER THREE

THE WRITING WORKSHOP

Since I'd done it many times before, there was not much to prepare for the writing workshop. I tied my hair in a bun rather than my usual braid and put on a semi-professional outfit I had brought. The handouts were already in my carry-on in the trunk of the car. I didn't want to rely on technology in case there wasn't any.

The first thing I noticed when I drove into the high school parking lot was the sheriff's car and a large crowd of people. Chris, looking dapper in a light beige linen summer sports coat, his sleeves rolled back above his wrists, and his hair combed back very neatly, was talking to the deputy.

I took my roll-aboard with the materials out of the trunk and walked over to the entrance where a middle-aged woman of average height with a thin face and permed hair greeted me: "I'm Helen, the president of the Mountain Writers Club," she said. "Do you need any help carrying anything?"

"No, I'm good, thank you." I saw Chris was looking at me—what a handsome devil he was! I waved and walked into a state-of-the-art classroom, freshly painted in light beige with one calming light blue wall. Up front stood a console with a computer and a document camera, similar to what we had at our college. Helen showed me how to turn everything on and how to pull down the screen.

"Only 20 people from the club will be allowed in, plus Mr. Cronin, who is here to observe," Helen explained.

"Oh, that's nice." I said and paused for a moment. "I'm amazed and appalled by the drug dealing that goes on around here and all the young students, children that have overdosed on heroin," I continued as I arranged my handouts on the table meant for that purpose.

"It's an epidemic, and that's why we have the deputy here," Helen said. "We want to make sure no dealers are around at the writing workshop tonight. The sheriff's department will monitor all events at the schools this summer."

People, mostly women but also a few men, drifted in and milled about before finding their seats at individual desks. Chris seemed to know everyone, who greeted him as either Chris or Mr. Cronin. Bits and pieces of conversation wafted over to me, and I heard Chris say, "No, it will never get any better." Was he ill? Did he suffer from an incurable disease?

"So, Chris, you're going to be a writer too now?" a young, plain but shapely woman of about thirty with short brown hair and dressed in a short brown skirt and brown boots asked Chris.

I could see blue veins popping out on Chris's forehead. "F.U, Annette," he sneered under his breath. "Why don't you mind your own business, huh?"

Chris had been careful to use polite language around me, but in his business, he was, of course, around a rough bunch of people.

"It's probably not necessary for me to stay around," he said to me. "But I'm here, so why not see what you can do?" He still sounded a little gruff.

"Yes, you might accidentally learn something," I said, maybe a bit sarcastically.

"You never know."

He found a seat in the back corner. I turned to the class and introduced myself. "And I assume you all know each other, so I'll learn your names and something about you as we go along." Then I talked a little about mystery writing as Helen had suggested when she invited me to do the workshop.

"How do you start?" was the first question as usual.

"From the back," I said. "Although you may introduce the murder right away. But you definitely need to know who the murderer is before you start. I have my highly intelligent and eccentric sleuth, an ex-nun turned psychology professor investigate and help the somewhat dull and clueless police. Then I need a group of plausible suspects to throw the readers off, and that's what I'm working on right now."

"What's it about?"

"A Chinese-American pianist and voice teacher who grew up in Chinatown in downtown Los Angeles has been found dead in a pool of blood in his Bunker Hill condo. And that's all I'm going to tell you, except that it's based on a true story, with information from news articles and police reports."

As I was talking, I passed out copies of "Oranges" by Gary Soto, a poem about a young boy who's going out on his first date. "Often the hardest thing is to get started on a story," I said. "And a good way to avoid writer's block is to use an article, a story, or—in this case—a poem, as a springboard." I asked a man in the front row to read the poem, which he did very well.

"Now think of your own first date. You can use some of the expressions in the poem if you like. That's not plagiarism, unless you copy whole stanzas." People started writing furiously. Chris too. "If some of you want to share your stories afterwards, we can do that."

I walked around the room and read over their shoulders. They seemed to have a lot to say. Some wrote about meeting their husbands for the first time; one wrote about a crush she had on a student in her algebra class in high school, and another wrote about going out on her first date with a guy who was sixteen while she was only fourteen. "His name was Eddie," she wrote. "And we were both in the marching band together. He was going to pick me up in his new car, and my mother was obviously worried, even though I had told her he was an Eagle Scout. When he came to the door, my mother, to my embarrassment, came outside with us to wave goodbye. That's when she saw Eddie's mother sitting in the back seat. The two mothers waved to each other, and I could see the relief on my mother's face." Very cute!

The classroom had a document camera, and I put up my own published story in response to the poem "Incident" by Countee Cullen, one of the Harlem Renaissance writers, who wrote about a brief encounter with a white boy in Baltimore. The boy called Cullen the N-word, and this little incident colored his whole stay in that city. I wrote about a time I had taken my friend's four-year-old daughter to a fancy Easter egg hunt in an upscale area where we were treated shabbily by a plain-looking lady who passed out drinks. She obviously thought we were a couple of ragamuffins who didn't belong in her fine society. The club members politely complimented me.

I looked over Chris's shoulder and read, "We met over broken sprinklers," he had written. "But unlike the girl in the poem, she had no rouge on her cheeks or gloves on her hands because she was a sporty type with a good body, big blue eyes, and golden unruly hair, so I called her Goldilocks. After I fixed the sprinkler heads, we had our first date over coffee. She's a little out of my league with all her degrees, but...."

He looked up at me innocently with a crooked, mischievous smile and a glint in his eyes. Blood rose to my cheeks. My face felt hot, and I turned away.

"You're making the teach blush, Chris," said the woman Chris had called Annette. An annoying woman for sure.

I asked for volunteers to share their stories, and many had produced good work. "Some of you may want to send your stories to small or big newspapers or magazines that publish guest commentaries. They may not pay you anything, but it's fun to see your stories in print."

People lingered after the session to talk to me, but soon only Chris and Annette remained. "How about a cup of coffee afterwards?" Chris suggested to me, but Annette answered, "Yeah, let's take the teach to the Lakeside Café for a treat."

"Sure," I said, and to Chris, "Can I come along in your car then since I don't know where to go?"

"Of course," Chris said and picked up my bag, took it to my car, and put it in the trunk.

"You go along, Annette. We'll meet you there."

"I can take the teach," Annette suggested.

"No," I said. "I'll go with Mr. Cronin."

"Okay, if you think that's safer."

Annette finally drove off, and Chris led me over to his car, a light brown, older model Range Rover, a popular car in Africa and similar to the car I had driven over there.

"Nice car," I said. "I used to drive a Range Rover in Africa. It got us through all the bad roads and lack of roads. Everything was really muddy when it rained."

"Yes, it's a good car in rugged terrain, but so is your little Subaru."

To my surprise, he didn't invite me to get in but just looked at me and said, "Do you mind if we don't go out for coffee?"

"Of course not," I said, although I couldn't understand what had made him change his mind.

"I really hate Annette. She's evil and has spread malicious rumors about me. She works for our small-town shyster lawyer, an equally bad guy who has made the most spiteful accusations against me. I'm surprised you haven't heard the gossip." He paused, and his expression was serious, even sad. "I can take you home and walk back to get your car afterwards."

"No, that's ridiculous. I can drive home."

"I'll drive behind you then and make sure you get home safely."

After he walked me back to my car, I drove slowly down the narrow roads flanked by tall pine trees. It was pitch black, and it looked like scary trolls might jump out of the deep, dark woods any time. Chris drove behind me up the driveway and got out.

"Can I invite you in for a cup of coffee *here* then?" I asked

"Can I take a rain check on that?" He walked me up the few steps to the door. "So, how did you like my story?" he asked.

"It was well written. Keep writing. I'd like to read the next chapter."

"How about you write how you'd like it to continue? You're the writer."

I looked at him again and wondered why this guy was not in a relationship and had to be set up by Cindy.

CHAPTER FOUR

HIKING THE SHORT TRAIL

The two workmen hammered and sawed diligently the following day and by late afternoon seemed to have finished the job except for the painting which they said had to wait until the wood dried. I went about my business but did little writing. Chris never showed up, but he came in his truck the following day around noon, and he had his dog with him: a beautiful dark-colored German shepherd with alert, pointed ears. "Hi," I said. "What a beautiful dog! What's his name?"

"It's a bitch," he said, "a female, and her name is Duchess. Say hi, Duchess." Duchess gave me one low bark. "I brought some snacks and thought we could go for a short hike," Chris suggested. "Have you hiked the short trail right off the highway by Vista Point? It's only about five or ten minutes from here."

"No, I've seen the sign, but I've never stopped to check it out."

"It's nice, you'll like it."

"Give me a few minutes to get my visor and some sunscreen."

When I returned, Duchess was in the narrow back seat of the truck, and Chris opened the passenger door for me. "Hop in," he said.

"She looks like a purebred," I said.

"Oh, yes, she's from a fine line, and she's very smart."

We drove off and parked by the small ranger shack at the head of the trail. Chris let Duchess loose, and she bounded down into the tangled shrubbery.

"Shouldn't she be on a leash?" I asked

"Oh, she'll come back when I call." He blew a whistle, and Duchess came racing back, wagging her tail wildly, and expecting praise and a treat which she got. I held out my hand and let her sniff around me. Then she was off again.

We walked down a soft path and stopped at a sign that informed us that the pine tree in front of us, which had its needles growing in bundles, was a Coulter pine. There were many other beautiful pines along the trail and also black oaks—which with their large leaves looked like the oaks growing in the Midwest, differing from California oaks that have smaller leaves. Signs abounded with interesting information about the fauna and flora in general.

"What spectacular views!" I pointed out as I stopped at a clearing with a view of a meadow. "These rangers or whoever marks these trails sure know how to pick the best spots."

"Maybe we could try a longer one tomorrow," Chris suggested. "It's Sunday, a time to take a break from work. Have you tried the trail out by the forest fire station?"

"No, is it very difficult?"

"It's more challenging than this one, but not that bad."

I had stopped at a grove of really tall pines and was surprised to learn that they were giant sequoias. "I didn't know sequoias grew in the San Bernardino Mountains," I said.

"They're actually not native to this area," Chris explained. "But they thrive here and blend in well among the sugar pines and cedars." He paused as if to listen. "Do you hear the woodpecker?"

I had stopped in front of another plaque which described yet another charming vista. There was a small, dry meadow below us surrounded by a thicket of brush and trees, and there was the red-headed woodpecker, working furiously on a tall pine tree. "How gorgeous this place is!" I said.

"'Beauty is in the eye of the beholder,' I think your friend Shakespeare said."

I looked up at him, and my eyes met his blue-green gaze. "I think a Greek philosopher may have said something similar a couple of thousand years earlier," I said as if I were correcting a student. "But Shakespeare may have expressed the same idea." I remained silent for a while. "Who needs church to communicate with God when you have this?" I said finally.

"Are you religious?"

"If you mean, do I attend church service every Sunday, the answer is no, but I consider myself spiritual. I believe there is a force out there, higher and more powerful than humans, but we're not equipped to understand it. What about you?"

"I'm not sure about organized religion either, but what you're saying sounds reasonable. I guess organized religion is better than unorganized religion as one pastor jokingly countered when he and I discussed the issue once." He moved closer, and I felt his heavy arm around my shoulder as he gave me a squeeze. I startled, but a warm current rushed through me. I didn't dare look at him, and not knowing what else to do, I just stared at the fallen leaves around my feet.

"I can give you a friendly hug, can't I?" he said. "I'm not going to hurt you."

"Yes, of course. You startled me, that's all." I moved closer and put my head on his shoulder to show him that I didn't mind.

"It's true what I wrote about you the other day," he said. "You seem a little unapproachable, but I like that." He smiled.

"I imagine you have many women throw themselves at you," I shot back teasingly.

"Not anyone I want," he said simply.

There was something innocent about him, something vulnerable too. I had the strange feeling he wanted someone to take care of.

We stood in silence a little while longer, enjoying the moment. At least I did, and I was afraid of my own feelings. I liked to be near him, and I liked to be around him, but I wasn't sure then how he felt.

"We should probably move along. Don't you have to get back to work?" I said and started down the trail ahead of him, stopping to read the signs.

At the trail head we sat down at a picnic table, and Chris went over to the truck to pick up the snacks. He called Duchess and gave her a dog biscuit first, and then he gave me a water bottle and a Nature bar. "Not much of a lunch," he apologized. "But I didn't have time to get sandwiches. Next time I'll have Maria make us some Mexican treats."

I was happy to hear there would be a next time.

"I guess I'd better get back to work," he said. "I have good people who can take charge, but I still have to let them know I'm around."

We went back to the car, and we drove back to my cabin. Nothing more was said about our next tryst, and I wondered where this relationship was going.

CHAPTER FIVE

SOME OF THE MYSTERY REVEALED

That Sunday morning, Chris and Duchess returned in his Range Rover. I had braided my hair especially tight and had put on my good hiking boots as well as extra sunscreen. We drove over to the forest fire station about half an hour from the resort and seemingly in the middle of nowhere. As Chris was busy parking across the highway from the fire trucks, a healthy brown bear and her cub lumbered down the path in front of us to disappear behind the bushes and trees. "Maybe this isn't the best time to hike this trail," I suggested. "I think I'll stay in the car."

Chris laughed. "They won't bother us," he said. "But we'll first take the short trail on the other side of the road and see how the Serrano Indians spent their summers."

"What if there are bears over there too? I don't want to test my strength against a mother bear with her cub."

"No, there are only oak trees over there, and bears like pines."

"Yeah, right! Where did you learn that?"

"No, it's true. Come on."

We left the food in the car, put Duchess on the leash, and crossed the highway. Another spectacular trail lay ahead of us. A little way down, a bronze plate on a small monument explained how the Indians ground acorns into a meal in small *metates* or milling stones, hollows in the flat granite rocks that surrounded a golden meadow. The Indians probably made acorn pancakes that they ate with wild berries. There were acorns everywhere, and I picked up a few and tried to grind them in a hole in one of the boulders. I gave some of the ground meal to Chris, but he spat it out. "It tastes terrible," he said.

"Squirrels like it," I said teasingly and tried some, but it tasted bitter.

Despite the drought, a purling brook cut through the area, and the serene and beautiful scene looked like an idyllic nineteenth century landscape painting.

We covered the short trail quickly and returned to the car. "We'll take water, but we'll leave the food in the cooler locked up in the car until we get back. No need to tempt fate," Chris said.

The trail was long and rocky, and although we stopped for frequent water breaks, we made steady progress upward toward the pinnacle. I soon felt perspiration run down my back and was happy when I could finally plunk myself down on a large rock shaped like a love seat on the pinnacle itself. There was no one else around. Chris sat down on a rock opposite me before he let Duchess loose and checked his phone for messages.

"Can you get reception all the way up here?" I asked.

"Yep, the fire station is not that far away, and there is also a recycling plant nearby too. We actually passed it."

"That's amazing. I didn't notice it. It seems so deserted out here."

"Yeah, the plant is well hidden."

The view was spectacular, and we could see the endless high desert for miles around us, a dry and desolate landscape. Chris rattled off the names of some mountain peaks. He was clearly a nature lover and an outdoorsman.

"You're pretty sporty," he said as he came over and sat next to me. I tried to brush some loose hairs back and checked if my braid was coming apart. "This isn't an easy hike, and you're not as used to the altitude as I am." He gave my braid a tug. "I like your French braid,"

"It must be messy right now."

"No, it looks fine. I know how to make a French braid too, you know. And I can do a fishtail too."

"Really? Where did you learn that?"

"I had a little girl once."

"You *had* a little girl? What happened to her?"

"She died three years ago."

"Oh, my God! I'm so sorry. "

"No, it's all right. It was for the best. She had Down's syndrome. She had a weak heart too, and when she got double-sided pneumonia, she had to go to the hospital, where she died of a heart attack. She loved it when I fixed her hair, so I had to learn to braid her hair different ways. And her hair was thick and golden too, but not quite as golden as yours." His tone was melancholy.

It was my turn to put my arms around him and give him a hug. "What about her mother? She must have had a mother."

"Sorry, that's a long story, and I'll tell you all about it another time."

"What was your little girl's name?"

"Emily, and she was very cute and so funny sometimes."

"So, we've both lost someone close to us." I said, stunned. Of course, I had expected that he too must have been married or had a serious relationship, but why couldn't he tell me about it? This woman, this absent mother, was obviously no longer in the picture, so she must either be dead, or they were divorced, and divorce is not a big deal today, I thought.

I don't remember how long we sat there, gazing at the vast landscape all around us, like Adam and Eve in Milton's *Paradise Lost* after the two sinners left the Garden of Eden with the world all before them and Providence their guide. Despite a chilling wind, I didn't feel particularly cold and time appeared to stand still, at least for a while.

"We should probably move along," I finally said. "The wind is starting to blow up dust, and soon it will be colder."

"Don't you think I'll be able to keep you warm?" he said with that special glint in his eyes again. "But I guess not. You must be hungry too." Fortunately, he was already back to his lighthearted self.

"A little," I said as I rose and started down again.

It was late afternoon when we got back to the car, and Chris took out ham and cheese sandwiches. "So, your housekeeper makes sandwiches for you too," I said. "Or are these the Mexican treats you said she was going to make for us today?"

"She does cook for me, but she doesn't come on Sundays, and I forgot to tell her yesterday, so I made these myself."

"They're delicious," I said after I had taken a bite.

"I'm glad you like them because it's the best I can do." He took out his phone again and checked his emails, voicemails, or whatever.

"Do you need to check in even on a Sunday?" I asked, a bit annoyed.

"One of my men fell down from a second-story deck at one of our job sites yesterday. He had to be brought to the hospital in an ambulance, and I asked his son to update me as soon as he had any news."

"I'm sorry. He must have broken some bones."

"We don't know yet. Maybe we won't know until tomorrow. Hopefully, it's not his neck or back that's injured."

His concern for his workers impressed me.

When we arrived back to my cabin, Chris got out but left Duchess in the car. He said he wanted to take a look at the new shed door. "It looks good, doesn't it?" he said.

"Yes, great, but they're not quite finished, are they?"

"No. they'll prime and paint and finish the steps this week."

"Actually, I have a problem with an electric outlet in one of the upstairs bedrooms too," I said.

He looked at me inquiringly as we walked inside and up to the third level of the cabin. "Oh, that's dangerous," he said when he saw the big hole in the wall and the loose cover plate hanging by the wires. "Don't touch it. I'll have an electrician come over and fix it this week."

I showed him the leaky bathtub and the cracked mirror too, but he suggested that that could wait. "We have more time in the late fall and winter," he said.

As we walked down to the middle level and passed my bedroom, he stopped. "You sleep in that big king-size bed all by yourself?" he said. "That seems a real waste, doesn't it?"

"True. Do you have any suggestions?"

"I might come up with something," he said jokingly, but he did not try to make any more advances, although I would have been easy prey at that time.

Instead, we had coffee on the deck, and it was just after sunset when he left.

CHAPTER SIX

WEEKEND VISITORS

Over the next two days I wrote profiles of two more suspects in my mystery novel. I didn't see Chris, but an electrician came to fix the outlet in the upstairs bedroom, and the two guys came to finish the steps and prime the shed door. The next afternoon, when I was out sweeping leaves off the driveway again, Chris came walking up from his work site down the road.

"How's the job coming?" I asked

"It's slow right now. Do you want to come and take a look?"

We walked down to the large compound of buildings. This was surely a big job.

"The main house was flooded by the firefighters as they were battling the out-of-control fire," he explained again. "But now the new windows are in, the plumbing and electrical lines are in place, and the walls are up and painted too."

"It's going to look nice," I said.

"Yeah, but it's a long way from finished."

We walked around the house and looked at the new flooring as well. To my untrained eye, everything looked expertly done.

"How much do you make on a job like this one?" I asked.

"Oh, there's a good profit on this one," he said. "An insurance company in Monrovia is paying for all the work. The owner of the property has a manufacturing business down in Riverside, not too far really, but I believe he said he lived permanently in Beverly Hills."

Afterwards, we walked around the short loop of roads back to my place, where I made coffee that we took out on the deck.

"I wanted to tell you that I'm finally ready to take my boat out on the lake this Sunday," Chris said. "Do you want to come along? My brother with his wife and son will be there, and maybe my sister-in-law's sister and her husband."

"Oh, I didn't know you had a boat," I said. "I'd love to come. What time?"

"I'll pick you up around two or so. How's that?"

"That should be fine," I said. "I have some friends from school coming up this weekend, but they'll leave on Sunday shortly after noon. They're teaching summer school and have to be at work early Monday morning."

"What are you going to show them?"

"On Saturday, I plan to take them to that short hiking trail off the highway that you took me and Duchess to last weekend, and then we'll probably go down to the resort for coffee and some shopping. You're welcome to join us in the evening if you have time."

"We'll see. I probably won't have much to talk to them about unless they need some work done on their houses. And I might not be able to keep up when you discuss obscure works by Shakespeare and other literary themes that I don't know anything about."

"Don't be ridiculous," I countered and slapped him on his arm in protest. "We talk about many other things too. And by the way, I may not have much to talk about with your brother and his wife either."

"My sister-in-law Elizabeth is a teacher too," he said. "She teaches math at the high school, and her sister Cheryl is a nurse."

"Oh, that's interesting. Maybe we'll have something in common after all then."

"What exactly do your friends do?"

"Kevin, the young one, is a freshly minted PhD and an expert on modern American literature. He's still in his twenties, and he's only taken the job with us as a stepping stone to something bigger and better. Alan is older, maybe in his late forties, and knows everything there's to know about Shakespeare. Susie is an attractive woman, just a little older than I am, with long auburn hair and a beautiful face. She's an opera buff like myself, and we've sometimes traveled together. She's divorced—her ex-husband is a doctor—and they have a daughter, Ashley. All four of us teach literature and writing."

"So you like opera?" he said. He sounded a little surprised.

"I don't like *all* operas, but I enjoy live productions of the major ones."

"I don't know anything about it," he said apologetically. "It sounds like a bunch of people screaming at the top of their lungs in Italian or some other language. I guess I really don't understand it. The sound of cows dying in the driveway comes to mind."

Robert hadn't cared for opera either, or classical music in general for that matter. He would come with me to performances if I asked him, but he was happy when I had someone else to go with.

"Maybe we could go together sometime to see a good one, something like *Aida* or *Carmen*. They are easy to understand, and the music is great."

He nodded thoughtfully. "Yeah, that should be interesting."

On Friday evening Kevin, Alan, and Susie arrived about six. They brought several bottles of wine, and I had spaghetti and meatballs ready for them on the deck, not exactly mountain fare, but something that was easy to prepare ahead of time. Alan's hair looked blonder and wavier than last time I saw him. He must have had a new color job and a cut. Kevin's short, black stick-up hair made him look very hip and young. Susie had her hair covered by a blue baseball cap.

"What's new at school?" I asked after we had all admired the view.

"Nothing much," Kevin said. "The old biddies sit around with sad faces looking at spreadsheets and flowcharts, making projections and talking about assessment, rubrics, the new platform, beta testing, metadata, and more assessment. If regular people were to listen in on all this crap, they'd think we were stark raving mad."

We nodded in agreement and had a good laugh before he continued: "And as usual good old Dr. Hertz, the sly fox, tosses the jargon right back at them and has them charmed."

"Yes, Dr. Hertz certainly is a charmer," I said. "And, behind their backs he chuckles and makes fun of them."

Of course, I told them about Chris, how we met over broken sprinklers, the writing workshop, and what he'd written in his paper, our hikes, and his slow advances.

We stayed up late and slept in Saturday morning. After breakfast we went on our hike and enjoyed the spectacular beauty of the place. We didn't see Chris until we walked back from the resort and passed by the fire-and-water-damaged house down the road.

"Chris, come and meet my friends," I called out to him, and he came over and shook hands with everyone. He called Alan, who was taller and about ten or fifteen years older than Chris, "Sir," and, as seemed to be his style, he took charge of the situation in a friendly and jovial way as if he were selling them a remodeling job.

"We've brought sandwiches from the resort," I said. "Can you join us?"

"I'd better finish up here," he said and gave us all the old line about how contractors in the mountain had to work in the summer when all of us were off. But he may have seen the disappointment on my face because he quickly added, "I'll come up afterwards for coffee and a goodnight kiss. How's that?"

"That's better," I said.

"He has the looks," Alan commented as we walked on. Ever since he'd been the theater director at the college, he was constantly on the look-out for handsome people, potential actors that he could cast in his plays. His wife of many years, who was now in Texas visiting her wheelchair-bound mother, was pleasant enough but rather plain.

"He does run his own contracting business pretty well though, Alan," I said defensibly. "So it's not all about looks."

Chris did stop by later.

"Did you have anything to eat?" I asked.

"Yeah, the guys brought up something from the 7-Eleven store. Coffee will be fine." Addressing the others, he said, "So, what do you think of our little resort town in the mountains?"

"It's absolutely beautiful," Susie said. "Have you lived here long?"

"I grew up here, but after high school I lived in New York for a while. My father thought I needed to see a little of the world."

"What did you do there?" Susie wanted to know.

"I studied engineering at New York University, but I didn't like it. Too much booze and drugs and shitty parties; so I came back here after a year and worked in the family business before I went out to Arizona State. Lots of parties there too, but I finally learned to stay away from the party scene and got a business degree."

"Yes, Arizona State is reportedly the number two party school in the United States, after San Diego State," Alan said. "But NYU is a hard place to get into," he continued. "You must have had pretty good grades in high school."

"They were okay, but Arizona State was a lot easier."

"With your looks, I'm surprised they didn't put you on stage," Alan said bluntly.

I wondered what play he had in mind for Chris.

Chris looked down and didn't seem amused.

"That's enough, Alan," I said, and to Chris, "Don't let it go to your head."

"I won't," he said flatly.

Kevin quickly changed the subject. "And now I understand you build houses," he said.

"Yep, and other things too, like decks, parking structures, and even some remodeling jobs. Unfortunately, it doesn't give me much time for anything else. Not much time for Shakespeare." He looked at me as if to make sure I was paying attention. "Actually, I took a Shakespeare class once, but I'm sorry to say it wasn't the most interesting class I've ever taken. I guess I'm more into reading manuals and material specifications."

"Most teachers don't know how to teach Shakespeare," Alan said. "To just sit and read Shakespeare's plays can be deadly." Alan was in his element now, lecturing a novice on his favorite subject. "I've made a pact with myself never to have students *read* plays again. Today, students watch DVDs of famous performances with top-notch actors, and in class we include film clips of memorable scenes. Only then can we have a lively discussion."

"There's more to life than literature," Susie broke in as she looked at Chris and then at me. We both noticed that Chris's eyes had started to glaze over. Susie always had the knack for saying the right thing.

"Alan used to be a wrestler, you know," I said to Chris. "He's not all about books."

"Really? I never tried that myself," Chris said. "But we have a good wrestling team at the high school right now. I used to play baseball and football."

He and Alan expounded on the topic of sports while drinking their coffee. After they had exhausted the subject, Chris said, "Tomorrow, Megan and I are taking my boat out on the lake. Maybe next time you come up, you can stay longer and come out with us."

"That would sure be a treat," Alan said.

"We won't be quite so busy later on in the summer," Chris explained as he finished his coffee and got up to leave. "See you later, Goldilocks. I'll pick you up tomorrow at 2 o'clock. Nice meeting you all."

I walked him downstairs, thanked him for coming, and gave him a quick kiss on the cheek.

"Goldilocks?" Kevin teased as I came upstairs again.

"Yes, it's pretty silly," I said. "But now, if you're finished with your coffee, let's have some of the good wine you brought." I got out a bottle and again we stayed up late.

As a result, we got a late start again on Sunday. The trio was preparing to leave when a white sedan with a man and woman in the front seat and two boys in the back drove up the driveway. The driver rolled down the window.

"Hi!" I said. "Can I help you?"

"I've come to pick you up? Didn't Chris tell you? I'm Ed, Chris's older brother."

"Oh, so you must be the sheriff. No, he never told me."

"This is my wife Elizabeth. My son James and his friend Thomas are in the back."

Alan came over as Kevin and Susie were getting into the car. "Is everything all right?" Alan asked.

"Yes, this is Chris's brother Ed, the town sheriff." Then to Ed, "My friends are just leaving. Can you give me a minute while I grab my things?"

Alan said goodbye again and went back to the car as Kevin, always the smart-aleck, stuck his head out the window and called out to me, "You have a busy life up here. I thought you had come up to the mountains for some solitude, some quiet time, and some serious writing."

"That was the idea," I said. "But plans change. It will be quiet again tomorrow. Drive carefully." I smiled and waved as they headed down the driveway.

CHAPTER SEVEN

THE MYSTERY DEEPENS (BOATING ON THE LAKE)

I went inside, grabbed my bag, and got in the back seat next to the boys. "Hi!" I greeted them. "Are you ready for a swim?"

"Yep," James answered.

"And they'll water ski too," Elizabeth said as we drove off.

"You teach math at the high school, I understand," I said and then I turned to James, "Do you have your mother for a teacher?"

"No, but Thomas has had her."

"And she's a good teacher," Thomas said diplomatically.

"Is math your favorite subject then?"

"Kinda," they both answered.

"And you teach literature and writing at Pacifica Junior College and write books," Elizabeth said. "That's exciting."

"It's all right."

"I hope Chris is treating you right," the sheriff said.

"Yes, he's very nice,"

"He's had a rough couple of years," he said, but didn't elaborate beyond that.

I was determined to find out what these rough years had involved. True, he had lost his daughter, but there must be more to the story.

"I hear you have a heroin epidemic at the high school. Is that true?" I asked.

"Yes," James said. "I knew at least twelve of the students who died from overdosing."

"You actually *knew* twelve kids who overdosed on heroin?" I said shaking my head. "I can't believe it can be that bad. What's the sheriff's department doing about it?" I asked Ed.

"It's very frustrating," he said. "The forest around here is vast and provides good hiding places. The dealers are clever, and there are just too many of them. This summer we're mounting an offensive. There won't be any dealing in summer school, I can guarantee you that. I even had a deputy at your workshop the other day, as you know, but Chris, who knows everybody around here, said it was pretty quiet."

"That's right. I was surprised when I saw a sheriff's car in the parking lot at the school, and Chris said he had been asked to be a kind of security guard. Fortunately, everything seemed all right."

The car snaked its way downhill toward the lake; the closer we came to the water, the more expansive the properties were. We parked in a spot above the dock, and I could see Chris in a tank top and shorts with a cap on backwards holding back his unruly hair. He looked as though he could have been one of my students. The boys jumped out of the car and ran down to the dock. Another couple was already in the boat, and the boys joined them. The rest of us followed. Chris shook his brother's hand and gave Elizabeth a quick hug before greeting me with a hug too. "We'll have steaks when we come back," he said and pointed to the grill and a big cooler with the anticipation of a child waiting for Christmas. As he helped me onto the boat, I noticed a swirly, nondescript tattoo on his right upper arm and shoulder but nothing on his left arm.

"What a nice boat you have!" I said. It was a flat-bottomed boat with beige vinyl cushions and faux mahogany accents. It looked relatively new.

"Thank you. I'm glad you like it."

"I didn't think a flat-bottomed boat could pull water-skiers," I said.

"This one can; it has a big engine. This is actually the biggest-size boat they allow on the lake. Do you water-ski?"

"I used to on the lakes back in Wisconsin when I was in high school, but that was a long time ago."

"Do you want to try today?"

"No, not in front of all these people." I turned to the couple I didn't know.

"Oh, this is Cheryl, my sister-in-law's sister, and her husband Jonathan Day," Chris said. "Cheryl is a nurse, as I told you, and Jonathan is a successful investor like Chad Cohen, Cindy's husband."

We exchanged greetings. Then Chris started the engine and maneuvered the boat out of the dock. Once the boat was well out on the water, he let James take the wheel, and we circled the lake leisurely while Elizabeth and Cheryl eagerly told me about the famous people who owned properties along the shoreline. We dropped anchor a little way from a small island, and the boys jumped in the water.

"Do you want to swim too?" Chris asked me.

"I guess so. I have my bathing suit underneath." I slipped out of my sun dress and looked over at Chris as he wrestled off his tank top. "Oh, my God," I blurted out, horrified. "What's that big scar across your chest and abdomen?"

He looked down as if he had just discovered it and quickly covered it with his shirt again. "Oh, that's a scar from my fightin' days," he said.

The long, diagonal scar was actually quite red and swollen and didn't look that old. The area around it was shaved, making it even more prominent, like a bandolier. I glanced over at Ed and the others, who all looked away. Did the scar have something to do with Chris's back-story that nobody wanted to talk to me about? I had to find a way to discreetly uncover this mystery, but for now I realized that I had caused an awkward moment. "Can we swim to the island over there?" I asked Chris in an effort to change the subject.

"Yeah, but it's farther than it looks."

"I'll race you."

"You want to race me to the island, and you think you can win? Hah, that will be the day." He laughed.

"Okay, let's see some action," I said coolly. "Or are you all about words? Come on boys," I shouted to James and Thomas. "We'll race your uncle Chris to the island."

I dove in, and the boys soon came up beside me, but it took a while for Chris to catch up. However, it was soon evident that he was a powerful swimmer. I heard the cheering from the boat, and I swam as fast as I could. I'd been a fast swimmer in high school, but there was no way to out-swim Chris, who stayed right beside me until we reached the small, sandy beach on the island.

"I guess I should have known better than to compete with those arms," I said and squeezed his right bicep. He had taken off his tank top again, and I couldn't keep my eyes from the terrible scar. The boys walked along the sandy shoreline to explore. The middle of the island was covered by shrubbery and trees.

"You didn't do too badly yourself," Chris said. "You're a good sport."

We sat down on the warm sand to rest, and I lightly touched his terrible scar.

"You can tell me things, you know," I said. "I'm a good listener. I'm not some dumb twenty-year-old either. Whatever it is will not change the way I feel about you."

"Which is?" he said slowly and looked at me.

"Positive," I said. "I like you a lot and enjoy being around you."

"I'll tell you, but not today, okay?"

I thought about a student I had in a night class at an adult school once who couldn't account for a couple of years of his life. I was in graduate school then and curious, and I found out that he had been to prison in Nevada for two years and was home on probation. He had been told by the judge to stay in school or go back to prison. I don't know what he had done, but he too was a nice guy and quite handsome. Evidently he didn't have a car and walked to class, a distance of over 100 blocks, so I took him home many evenings.

He must have noticed me staring at him quizzically because, as if he were reading my thoughts, he suddenly said, "No, I'm not sick. I'm not impotent either, if that's what you think, and I've not been a guest of Uncle Sam."

I felt a little foolish. The brother of an appointed lieutenant sheriff in prison didn't make much sense.

"Have you ever seen a bald eagle around here?" I asked. "They're up here, I understand."

"Oh, yeah, but not in the summer. They come down from the north and winter here. Sometimes I see one in the tall trees around my house near the lake, and they're spectacular. After October, we can volunteer to count them at different locations around the lake. I've done it many times." He took my hand. "We'd better go back to the boat. You feel cold."

The boys were out of sight, but Chris and I swam leisurely back. The water was cold, colder than the ocean that I had become more used to.

"Well done, Megan," Elizabeth and Cheryl said as I climbed aboard. "Here's some warm cocoa, but you better dry off first," Elizabeth said.

She gave me a towel that I wrapped around my shoulders and drank the hot cocoa. Chris already had his shirt on and was drinking something too, but I don't think it was cocoa.

"I'll hold the towel up so you can change out of your wet bathing suit and put on your dress. You don't want to catch a cold." Cheryl offered.

"I guess I'd better listen to the nurse," I said.

"That's right. Do you want some snacks?"

I took some cheese and crackers from a tray as it was passed around. Then I took out my hair brush and my Tangle Free® no-rinse hair conditioner and started on my unruly hair.

"Come over here," Chris said. "I'll help you untangle that mass of curls."

I sat down between his legs, and he went to work with my brush more expertly than I expected. I realized he had probably sat right there combing his little girl's hair, and I might very well be a substitute for this child. He had told me that he used to fix her hair too. In fact, working on my hair may have been a kind of therapy for him, and I wondered if the others were thinking the same. "You have experience, I see," I said.

"Chris has a lot of surprising skills," Ed said. "You're in for a treat with this handsome guy." He paused. "I'll call the boys back," he said to Elizabeth and called out in a booming voice. "We've promised them that they can ski around the lake a few times too. Can you help them, Chris?"

"Okay, the tangles are almost out."

"I need to cut it," I said. "It's too difficult to manage."

"Oh no, don't do that. You just need some good hair conditioner, that's all."

The boys came back, ready to water-ski. Chris was in the water with James first and got him started. Ed was at the wheel, and we took off, cheering as we cruised around the lake a couple of times before it was Thomas's turn.

When we finally returned to the dock, Chris fired up the grill, and we had New York steaks, potato salad, and a green salad with beer and wine and soft drinks for the boys. The air was a little chilly, and I was glad I had brought the little jacket that went with the dress.

The boys wanted to leave as soon as they finished eating, and everyone started to say goodbye.

"You're the best thing that could have happened to my little brother," Ed said softly, and the others quietly agreed. "But you two have a lot to talk about," he said to Chris. Chris looked down, and the blue veins popped out on his forehead again.

"I know," he said almost inaudibly as they were leaving. He didn't look at me and just sat there for a while in a cloud of gloom. "Do you want a beer?" he finally asked without looking up.

"I don't really drink beer," I said. "Are there any soft drinks left?"

"There's wine."

"Okay, I'll take a glass of wine."

He stood up, handed me a plastic glass, and poured the wine. I sat down and watched him pack the rest of the food in the cooler and tie up the garbage bag that the others had helped fill with plastic plates and left-over food. Then he sat down and downed another can of beer. When it was empty, he crushed it with one hand before he threw it toward the already full garbage bag.

"So, there won't be a story tonight then?" I said.

"Can I just have a couple of days to prepare my speech?" he asked.

"That's ridiculous. I don't know what the big deal is."

"It *is* a big deal. When you learn the truth about me, you may not want to speak to me ever again."

"That's even more ridiculous."

"It isn't." He put his head in his hands.

"I should probably be going now," I said finally. "I can walk. It's not that far."

"No, I'll take you home." He got up and picked up the cooler, and as we were walking up to his car that was parked in the driveway of a beautiful mansion, he said, "Now you're upset with me, aren't you?"

"Maybe."

It was getting dark, and I didn't pay much attention to where we were. He left the chest on the side of the driveway before we got in the car and drove the few minutes to my cabin in silence. It was as if a dark cloud had settled around us. I was tired, and when I walked into the cabin after a quick goodbye, I went straight to bed and slept late the next day. When I woke up the next morning and my head had cleared, I realized that if I wanted to continue this relationship, it was going to be on Chris's terms, and I regretted my pouting the night before.

At noon I gave him a call as he usually took a break for lunch. He answered right away.

"I'm sorry I was cross last night," I said. "I had a wonderful time swimming and hanging out with your brother and family, and I had no right to give you a hard time. And by the way, I believe I have another leaky sprinkler. Can you come by and take a look at it?"

I heard him chuckle. "It can probably wait until tomorrow. I'm down the hill in Redlands, and when I come up, I have to try to get the men to finish up before the storm that's forecast for tomorrow afternoon or Wednesday. We may have thunder and lightning too, so fasten all your windows and doors. Check the new shed door too, to make sure the guys locked it properly. When we have weather in the mountains, even in the summer, it can be bad."

"Okay, thanks. See you when you get here."

After I hung up, I sat motionless for a while, wondering what this guy really wanted with me.

CHAPTER EIGHT

INTIMACY

Dark clouds were gathering in the west all morning, and a few raindrops had started to fall when Chris came over in the early afternoon. I ran out to meet him as he got out of his truck.

"You're happy to see me?" he said as if he were surprised. His tight tan golf shirt showed off his strong shoulders.

"Yes, why? Shouldn't I be?"

"Well, yes, it's good. I took the boat out this morning and caught a rainbow trout that Maria is fixing for a late lunch. Care to join me? I've sent the guys home for the rest of the day."

"That would be nice. I haven't had lunch yet either. I'll just run in and get my purse and a sweater." I hurried inside and grabbed my things. Then I got in the truck beside him.

"I hope you like Mexican cooking. Maria has her own way of preparing trout."

"She really takes good care of you, doesn't she?"

"Yes, and she has three grown sons and a husband to take care of at home too, but she never complains. She's been with us since shortly after my mother died."

We parked in the same driveway by the same beautiful house I had barely noticed on Sunday night. "This is your house?" I asked in disbelief.

"Yes, you saw it the other night."

"Yes, I know, but I didn't pay much attention to it. This is not a cabin, it's a mansion."

"Not really. Let's go inside before we get all wet."

The inside matched the outside with high vaulted ceilings and wood-paneled walls decorated with old oil paintings of mountain motifs. On the opposite wall from the entrance hall was an oversized stone fireplace with a huge couch in front. The small windows made the room now look dark. Apart from an older grand piano that turned out to be a Steinway over on the side, the heavy furniture was made of solid oak, so appropriate for a mountain residence.

"It's gorgeous," I said.

"I'm glad you like it. My father built it after his business took off in the 1970s. I'll give you a tour."

From the big living room, we walked into the master bedroom, which had a king-size bed.

"You sleep alone in this big bed?" I asked teasingly. "It seems like a waste, doesn't it?"

He grinned. "Yeah. I'm sure we could put it to better use."

The master bedroom had its own bright and exquisitely tiled master bathroom, and the big country kitchen had all the latest stainless-steel appliances, A short, middle-aged woman was busy preparing lunch. She had a round, pretty face and short, curly black hair. Although stout, she was not fat and had a spring in her step as she bounced around in soft white leather shoes of the kind that nurses used to wear. A table for two was set in the cozy eating area on the side. She looked at me and smiled.

"Maria, this is my new friend and client, Megan Viets. Megan, this is Maria, my loyal and lovely housekeeper."

"Hi, Maria," I said.

"Nice to meet you, Miss," she said in a slight Spanish accent. Chris had mentioned she was originally from Mexico.

I was equally impressed with the dining room that had an oversized chandelier and a large oak table that could seat twelve. From there we went out on the large deck with a sweeping view of the lake below. He also showed me his gym, which featured different exercise equipment, and he showed me how to use the different machines. After working out for a few minutes, I inspected the small office scattered with papers, pictures of houses, and folders. In her own pen on the side of the house,

Duchess ran up and down in great excitement, and in the garage, Chris showed off three classic cars.

"This one is the same model that President Franklin D. Roosevelt used to drive," he said. "It's a Packard 1929. The other big one is a 1932 Chrysler Imperial and the little red sports car is a 1952 Allard."

"I've never heard of or seen an Allard before, but I know Packard and Chrysler, and the Packard looks like the car Roosevelt was often photographed in."

We walked around all of them, but at the time I didn't know anything about old cars, let alone classics.

"The garage is insulated and climate-controlled," he explained. But when he realized I wasn't impressed, we went upstairs, where he showed me more bedrooms and bathrooms and a sitting room that opened up on another deck with a great view of the lake. The large room had a big-screen television set and comfortable seating.

"Maybe we could relax and watch a movie after lunch," he suggested, and I agreed.

"You must be a really good contractor, Chris. This is a real treat."

"The company made money when we did highway construction for the Government," he explained again. "That's where I got started. Now we do more home and also industrial construction. We have some heavy equipment that we mostly rent out to other contractors, and we're still doing okay," he stated matter-of-factly.

Downstairs, Maria announced that lunch was ready, and Chris thanked her. "You'd better go home before the thunder and lightning start," he told her as he gave her a quick hug and some money. Then he sent her on her way.

"Have a seat at the table," he said invitingly. He got out a bottle of white wine from a built-in wine cabinet and poured it as I sat down. The meal was delicious, and we took our time.

"I'll make coffee and clear the dishes," he said. "We can bring the coffee into the living room."

Suddenly, the first lightning bolt struck the lake, followed closely by a roaring thunder clap. The electricity went out, and the room darkened.

"That's the end of the coffee for today," Chris said and started unplugging appliances. "And that's the end of our movie plans too."

I walked into the oversized living room and admired the big fireplace and the old paintings of nature scenes with bears, coyotes, bald eagles, finches, and other birds native to the area. But I had an eerie feeling that something was not as it should be, that I didn't belong here. The feeling was augmented by ghostly shadows created by the frequent lightning bolts that brightened the room momentarily; then followed by claps of thunder. Water streamed down the small windowpanes, blocking any view of the outside, and the stormy weather also created intermittent creaking noises. I shivered.

I went over to the grand piano and played a few chords. Not surprisingly, because it was an American-made Steinway, considered by many to be the most highly prized pianos in the world, the sound was good. It was out of tune, but not that bad for an old piano.

On one of the end tables, I noticed a picture of Chris with his arms around his little girl, and I went over to look at it more closely. There was no sign of a mother or any wedding pictures, however. Robert and I had tried to conceive at least the last three years of our marriage, but nothing happened. Now it was probably too late, and it was okay. I had my career and friends. That was good enough.

I was lost in my own thoughts and didn't hear Chris come up behind me, so I startled and stood petrified for a second or two when I felt his arms around me like a vice. I felt his hot kisses on the back of my neck, and the fear quickly evaporated, and I had no willpower to resist. He gently turned me around and started kissing me on the face and mouth. As I put my arms around him and kissed him back, I felt his erection. A sense of excitement rushed through my body, and I pulled him even closer. His closeness felt good. After all, I hadn't had any sexual encounters with anyone since Robert died. Chris pushed me toward the couch and unbuttoned my blouse and loosened my pants that slid to the floor. Then he removed my bra and underwear before he undressed himself.

Outside the storm was raging with more lightning strikes and thunder, but I hardly noticed it, and in the darkened room I didn't even notice Chris's scar. He pushed me down on the couch and lay down on top of me, and I felt him between my thighs first. Then he slipped into me.

Afterwards, I lay on his arm and traced my fingers along the scar as I listened to the storm. His body was warm. Everything felt so right and wonderful, and I didn't want to spoil the moment by perhaps saying the wrong thing again. I hoped he wouldn't recite the usual clichés, although, just in case, I was prepared with some of my own clichés. I wondered what his secret was, but at that moment I really didn't care. It couldn't be that bad. Little did I know!

"Do you want to take a shower with me?" he asked suddenly.

"Well, I guess," I said and then more assuredly, "Why not?"

He took my hand and led me into the luxurious and brighter bathroom and turned on the shower. We both stepped in for a good rinse, and then he got soap out and lathered my body completely. We laughed and giggled like a couple of teenagers, and I felt my wedding band sliding off my finger and falling on the hard tiles with a soft ping, I picked it up and put in the soap dish.

"Do you want me to wash your hair?" he asked.

The question was so innocent and matter-of-fact, but it took me by surprise. I had a colleague once, a teacher, whose husband was a commercial pilot, and he washed and blow-dried her hair every night when he was home, she said. Maybe that wasn't so unusual, although Robert would never have thought of it unless I was sick and asked him. Again, I wondered why he had an obsession with my hair, but maybe working on my hair was some kind of therapy for him. He had said he liked to fix his little girl's hair. "If you want to," I said. "Do you have shampoo and conditioner?"

"Is this okay?" he asked, holding up a drugstore brand of both shampoo and conditioner.

"Sure."

He massaged my scalp, then rinsed and conditioned my hair expertly. I saw his erection again, and he pushed me up against the wall, and we had another round. I had to marvel at his stamina.

"It's been so long," he whispered afterwards.

"For me too," I said. "It truly feels good to be with a man again. I haven't been with anyone since my husband died."

He appeared to think about that for a while.

"I had to have you at least once before you abandon me," he said finally. "And I can't believe how compatible we are. I know I need to level with you. I owe you an explanation, especially after today, but can it wait until tomorrow?"

"Yes, it's okay. I don't really care." Of course, I was a bit annoyed that he brought it up at this happy moment, but I thought whatever was on his mind couldn't be that bad, unless he was dying or something.

"I don't feel like taking you home," he said. "You belong here with me now."

"So that I can be your sex slave?" I said jokingly.

"Ooooh! I didn't see you putting up much resistance."

"You're right. I didn't mean to say that. You were wonderful, and I'm happy I've hooked up with you."

"Do you want to spend the night here?"

"Well, maybe not tonight. I didn't bring anything with me, and I don't think I locked my doors."

"I heard you play the piano, and it sounded nice. Do you want to play some more, or is it too much out of tune?"

"It's not that bad, but it needs tuning and looking after."

"We'll get a tuner from the guild in San Bernardino up here. I don't think it has been worked on since my mother died."

"I'll bring some music up here next time I go back to Los Angeles," I said.

Outside, it was almost completely dark, and the electricity had not come back on.

"Let's see if we can find something else to eat," he said as he lit several candles. We looked through the fridge and found eggs and cheese. He had a gas stove, so I scrambled eggs, and we had bread and more wine to go with it.

The rain had finally diminished to a drizzle by the time he took me home. He walked inside with me to make sure the electricity was on, and there were no leaks around the windows and doors. I put my arms around him and thanked him for taking care of me; and we just stood there for a minute or two, but soon he let me go and we said goodbye.

I got ready for bed alone.

CHAPTER NINE

A DRUNKEN EPISODE

He called every morning the next couple of days to see that I was all right, but I didn't see him again until Saturday night. It was well after dark when I noticed the headlights of a car coming up the driveway. I ran downstairs to greet him, but he didn't get out of his truck right away, so I walked over to see what was going on. I looked at him as he opened the door and struggled to get out, and I thought for a short moment that he was hurt, but then I smelled alcohol. His face looked puffy and red in the lamp light. "You're drunk," I said.

"I've had a few drinks, yes," he said as he tried to stand up. "I got the job for the school district in Redlands, and the guys wanted to take me out for a drink. It means steady work for them for weeks, even months, you know."

"That's nice. Congratulations," I said. "But how can you drive like this?"

"My brother is the sheriff, remember?"

"I know, but you could have been killed, and you could have killed other people too."

"They know to stay out of my way."

"So, this is a frequent occurrence with you then?"

"Goldilocks, don't be angry with me. Help me get up."

"My name is Megan," I said coldly as I pulled him up and offered him my shoulder so he could lean on me. "Come on upstairs, and I'll make some coffee to sober you up."

He struggled up the stairs. "No wonder you're in such good shape, running up and down these stairs every day," he lamented.

He walked over to the couch and slumped down. I went into the kitchen to make coffee.

"Come here and have a drink with me, Goldilocks," he said.

"Megan," I said.

"Okay, Megan." He pulled out a flat silvery flask from his shirt pocket, but I grabbed it before he could take another sip.

"I had to fortify myself before I could make my confession to you," he said. "My brother told me I need to be straight with you."

"You don't owe me anything," I said untruthfully. "And I don't want a serious speech while you're drunk. I'll get the coffee."

"But I want you," he said and held out his hand as I walked toward the kitchen. I paid no attention to him until I returned.

"Here I come," I said, trying to be funny as I set his cup on the coffee table. "Coffee, tea, and me?"

His eyes had closed, and he fell back on the many soft cushions I had made one summer. He was fast asleep before he had any coffee. I watched him for a while, and then I started to take his boots off. I soon realized that the couch was too small for him, and I tried to lift him up. He cooperated, and I steered him into the bedroom.

"I have to take a piss," he said and went into the bathroom. His filter was obviously down. How he had managed to drive from the resort along the narrow roads to my cabin I could not imagine. I guided him along to my bed, pulled back the cover, and undid his belt, unbuttoned his pants, and pushed him down. Then I removed his pants, took his car keys from his pocket, and put them in a box on my dresser in case he had any idea of getting up and driving away. Drunk as a skunk, he was soon gone, snoring like a sailor.

At a loss what to do, I wandered around the cabin, tidying up, watching the news, and finally getting ready for bed. I had intended to sleep in an upstairs bedroom but decided to lie down in my own bed. I was used to Robert next to me, but could I sleep next to Chris? I pulled the cover back and lay down quietly and looked at him. His face was flushed, and his hair needed brushing, but even in this disheveled state he was a handsome man. I carefully unbuttoned his shirt to look at his scar, but he had a tank top underneath, covering it up. Maybe he would reveal the mystery tomorrow.

I soon went to sleep and didn't wake up until the sun was high in the sky. Chris was stirring, but still asleep. He had probably worked hard to get the bid and needed rest. I got up quietly, made myself a cup of coffee, and went out on the deck. Sailboats and speedboats were already out on the dark blue lake. A busy woodpecker worked furiously on a tree below, and two squirrels scampered about trying to suck up a few drops of water from the sprinklers.

When I walked back inside, Chris was awake. He held out his hands, but when I bent over to give him a good-morning kiss, he groaned. "Careful. My head is being attacked by a sledgehammer."

"I'll get you a cup of coffee and a couple of aspirin," I said and went back into the kitchen. When I returned with the coffee and two pills, he was trying to sit up. "This will help you feel better," I said. "You can take a shower in my bathroom, but, sorry, there's only room for one. I'll make omelets and toast that we can have on the deck. It's a beautiful day."

"What happened last night? How did I get into this comfortable bed, and where did you sleep?"

"Right next to you. Remember, we didn't want this big king-size bed to go to waste."

"Thank you. I made a fool of myself, didn't I? What foolish stuff did I say?"

"Nothing, but I don't know how you managed to drive in that state all the way up here on these dark, narrow roads."

"I know these roads like my own pocket, remember? I can drive with my eyes closed around here."

"Don't try that again, please. I don't want to be a widow once more."

He smiled and said, "I won't." Then he got up with some effort and disappeared into the bathroom.

The omelets came out looking so-so, but they were good. Other than the woodpecker and some squawking blue jays, there wasn't a sound around.

"You have a great view of the lake," Chris commented. "It adds a lot of value to your cabin."

"It's not as nice as yours," I said.

"Well, my house is closer to the lake, but your view is just as good."

"Maybe if you have time after breakfast, you could show me another hiking trail."

"We could do that." He rooted around in his pockets. "Did you see my car keys anywhere?"

"Yes, I put them in a box on my dresser, but we can take my car if you don't want people to see that you're using the company car for hiking trips."

"Okay, I'll park the truck down at the work site. I don't want to ruin your reputation, although the damage may already have been done. How old is your Subaru?"

"About four or five years. It's a four-wheel drive."

"All the cars of that make have four-wheel drive. And it's a good mountain car."

"That's why we bought it."

"Your husband bought it?"

"Yes, I wanted a nicer color, but he said the dark green was more durable."

"Smart choice." He got his keys from the box and went down to move the truck while I put the dishes away and got ready. He had left his jacket on the couch, and I hung it on a hanger on the doorknob in the bedroom before I got my own car keys and went downstairs. I drove down to the work site, and Chris came up to the driver's side. "Do you want me to drive?" he asked.

"No, it's my turn today." I hoped he wasn't one of those guys who felt uncomfortable being in the passenger seat while his girlfriend was driving. If so, I certainly wanted to disabuse him of that notion early. He walked around and got in next to me. Before we started out, he gave me directions, and I drove up to a higher elevation and a trail overlooking the ski resort where Robert and I had often skied. Again I marveled at the trail blazers and their ability to find the most gorgeous spots.

We took it easy and rested often, watching and marveling at the big lizards darting across the granite rocks. Playful squirrels scampered about and jumped from tree to tree, while different kinds of birds soared overhead.

"I guess this weekend I have to tell you my sad story," he said after a while. "Otherwise my brother will come over and tell you himself. Ed said you're too nice to be kept in the dark."

"We can wait until we get back," I said.

"That's a good idea in case you get so mad at me that you tell me to start walking while you drive home by yourself."

"Don't be absurd. I'd never leave you to walk home."

He pointed out the different runs at the ski resort, a moderate resort with few really difficult runs, but fun and convenient since it was so close to the cabin.

I drove back as well; to Chris's chagrin I'm sure, because he was watching the road as if he were at the wheel.

"Are you afraid when other people drive and you're not in control?" I asked as we finally drove up my driveway.

"No, it's just that I know this area better than you do."

"Well, we got home safely."

"Yes, and you're a reasonable driver."

"Thank you."

CHAPTER TEN

THE BOMBSHELL

W e went upstairs and out on the deck. "I'll make coffee and fix us some snacks," I said.

"No, let's talk first. Sit down."

He sounded sincere, so I sat down obediently while he pulled up a chair and seated himself in front of me. He took both of my hands in his and looked me straight in the face with his mesmerizing eyes.

"What's this?" I asked. "Doom and gloom's day?"

"Megan, be serious. This is not a joke. Take a deep breath."

I did, and I started to feel uneasy. What could be so important? We were both alive and had a wonderful time together. What could destroy the happiness we both seemed to feel?

"Megan, you have known for some time that I have fallen in love with you," he began. "I don't need to say 'I love you' or anything like that because you know."

"Maybe," I said and had to admit to myself that I had fallen for him as well.

"And you have led me to believe that you care for me too, at least a little bit."

"Maybe," I replied again. He was, of course, quite perceptive.

"I didn't mean for this to develop so fast, but it has, and I need to level with you, put the cards on the table, and tell you the truth about me."

"You're making me nervous. What's going on? Please stop beating around the bush," I said apprehensively.

"Megan, I am married."

The words hit me like a ton of bricks. Blood rushed to my face, and I suddenly felt numb all over. I had known that all was not what it seemed, but this was not a variable I had thought of. "But where's your wife?" I finally asked. "She doesn't live with you because you said you lived alone with your dog, so why aren't you getting a divorce?"

"I am going to, of course. Trust me. But it's taking longer than I thought."

My face felt hot; I was sick to my stomach, and tears welled up in my eyes. "I need my hands to cover my face," I said in a shaky voice, trying to keep from crying.

"I'll give you one hand only," he said and held onto the other. "It's not as simple as you think. My wife is insane. She was institutionalized almost two years ago after she tried to kill me with a big kitchen carving knife. She missed my heart but pierced one of my lungs, and I was in the hospital for over two weeks. You've seen my scar."

Oh, my God, so that was the story about the scar. "Where's she now?" I managed to whisper.

"In the state mental hospital for the criminally insane in San Bernardino; the judge put a restraining order against her. She's not to come near me. As you already know, we had a daughter with Down's syndrome who died. I took care of her because her mother couldn't. I had to take care of both of them."

"How did you get involved with someone like that?" I asked quietly, trying to regain my composure.

"Yeah, I'm wondering about that myself sometimes," he said. "What was I thinking? I was a jerk." He paused. "But she wasn't always crazy. I knew her from high school, and she was pretty and sexy and smart too, back then, and her father was the town lawyer, so they had a certain status here in town."

"You don't seem like someone who cares about status," I said.

"I don't, but her father could have gotten me in trouble."

"How?"

"She was pregnant. I suspected that she had slept with other guys, but she told me no and that the baby was mine. And I know for sure it was true because Emily had a big mole on her back in the exact same spot as me."

"I see."

"So, I agreed to marry her, and at first it was fine," he continued. "The birth and the Down's syndrome triggered the onset of schizophrenia; which, I guess was always there, and when I think back, she was odd at times."

"That's terrible," I said. I was slowly starting to get interested in the whole sordid story. "My mother had a cousin with schizophrenia," I continued. "Her father, my mother's uncle by marriage, had it too."

"Yes, it's in their DNA. Both my brother and my father warned me against getting involved in that family. Her mother was crazy too. She left the father when Amanda, that's my wife's name, was in her senior year in high school." He sighed. "Schizophrenia can evidently be triggered by all kinds of things."

"Yes, I know." I was starting to feel sorry for him. "With my mother's cousin it happened at the onset of puberty. She was an A student, and suddenly her grades dropped, and she failed her classes."

"Yeah, that's what happens. When Emily died, Amanda went completely off the deep end. At the hospital she was diagnosed with psychotic schizophrenia, and there's no cure. Symptoms can be somewhat controlled with medication, that's all."

"I know."

"Of course, there was a lawsuit. My father found a good Jewish lawyer from Hollywood, who has a nice house on the lake up here as well. My father had done some work for him and knew him, and he was really good. We filed a lawsuit to get my wife committed. Then my father-in-law countersued and accused me of abusing my wife and causing Emily's death, but he didn't get anywhere." He paused to catch his breath. "I could go on and on. It was ugly, and you can imagine how the tongues were wagging in this small town. I'm surprised you haven't heard about it."

"I guess I really don't know many people around here. Cindy is not one to gossip."

"That's true. She's a good person," he said thoughtfully. "A lot different from Annette. You remember Annette from your workshop, right? She works for my father-in-law and is the worst gossip in town."

"Yes, I remember."

We both sat quietly for a while.

"You know I have a fair amount of assets," he went on. "And he's trying to fleece me."

"Who?

"My father-in-law. I know I have to take care of this wife for the rest of my life, but the money her father gets out of me won't go to her, and it irritates the hell out of me that he's the one getting it. Fortunately, the construction company is owned by the Cronin family trust as is the house and some rentals. My father was smart to see to that and also to keep himself as the principal trustee, but I have my own assets too. The cars that you saw are worth quite a bit, and I also have some rentals in my name, but never mind that now. I don't care. I want out." He looked at me imploringly.

"I'm so sorry," I said, and tears started to well up in my eyes again. "But none of this is your fault," I whispered after a while.

"I know, but it's still baggage that I have to carry around with me. I have a good lawyer, a young woman who graduated from Georgetown and then UCLA Law School, so she should be smart, and she specializes in difficult divorces. After Emily died and my wife was committed, I was really depressed."

"Well, that's understandable," I said. Actually, I don't know exactly what I said because I felt numb and couldn't think straight.

"I would wake up in the morning and wouldn't even want to get up," he continued. "Nothing gave me any pleasure. I wasn't interested in women, and I haven't had a serious relationship until I met you. Oh, maybe I had some one-night stands here and there, stupid women I had no real interest in. I started drinking too much too."

By now he was obviously determined to let it all out. I sat in disbelief, and it was really too much for me to absorb, but he went on: "My brother was a great help, and I worked out a lot in my gym, sometimes until I was so tired I couldn't think. And I did my own work alongside my guys, especially carpentry. I can still swing a hammer and use a saw, you know."

"You look so healthy and in shape," I said. "It's hard to imagine someone like you not being happy."

"I don't care about looks. There are more important things in life." He paused. "Your friend Cindy told me about you before you came up here, and when I saw you with your thick, golden French braid out on your walks, I fell in love with you from afar. I watched you when you passed the job site down the road, and when I drove by in my truck, you waved."

"I thought that's what you were supposed to do in the mountains," I said, trying to adopt a more lighthearted attitude again.

"We do," he agreed and then continued, "It was like falling in love with a phantom or an image, and when I met you in person, I was even more attracted to you than I could have imagined."

"So, the leaking sprinklers were just a set-up?"

"They were actually leaking but if they hadn't been, I would have found something else to fix for you."

"Well, your speech is certainly dramatic," I said, having by now pulled myself together. "Cindy said that you'd had a couple of rough years. Your brother said the same—and from what you're telling me *that* seems quite an understatement. But they also said that you were a nice guy."

"Thank God, the gossip never got to you."

"Well, I don't like gossip; I don't listen to gossip, and I haven't heard any gossip."

"That's good. I really respect Cindy, and I like her husband a lot too."

Chris was only a year older than I was, but he appeared so much more mature. He had certainly learned some life lessons. Maybe that's why he seemed so much more concerned for others than I was.

"And my biggest job now is to try to keep you with me," he concluded. "I won't let you leave me easily, you know." He smiled. "I've finally found someone that both my father and brother approve of too."

"That's good to hear, but I believe I'll have to go home for a few days, leave this little paradise for a while at least to clear my mind, to think all this through," I said. "I had actually planned to go home for a few days next week anyway."

"I thought the divorce would have been finalized by now. Unfortunately, it's more complicated than I thought, but it shouldn't be much longer now, according to my lawyer. Can you wait for me? Can we at least be friends until then?" He got up and pulled me up with him and held me tight before he let me go. "You probably want me to leave now," he said.

"Maybe." It was the only word I could get across my lips, and I felt sad. I realized that I'd been a little too gullible.

"But not before we've had something to eat," he said cheerfully. "Let's see what you have in the fridge."

He sat me down at the kitchen table and opened the refrigerator. The cool breeze from the open patio door made me shiver.

"You have a lot of salad material, I see. I'll whip you up a salad and maybe not coffee but something more soothing." He looked around the kitchen. "Hot cocoa," he said as he opened a cupboard door and saw a package of instant hot chocolate. He seemed genuinely concerned about me and the state that all of this had put me in—as if I was his little girl, and he had to take care of me.

The salad looked good, but I could only eat a couple of bites. The cocoa revived me some. "It will be good to go home for a few days," I said. "This place is such a fairy-tale land, and I lose touch with reality up here."

"But you'll be back?"

"Yes, that's my plan." I really didn't want to be alone again.

"You won't leave tonight though."

"No, I don't want to drive down the hill tonight and get home in the dark. I'll leave in the morning after rush hour."

"I'll call to make sure you get home safely. It's about a two-hour drive, right?"

"Yes."

"Don't judge me too harshly. If I'd told you everything the first time we met, would you have gone out with me?"

"I don't know. It's not your fault, and I do like to be around you."

"Do you think I should have waited until after you'd heard the gossip?"

"No, it's okay. I want to know, and I'm an adult woman, not a little girl that you seem to want to take care of."

He didn't say anything, but got up, ready to leave. I went downstairs with him and stood looking after him as he walked down to his work site to get his truck. When I went upstairs again, I saw that he had left his jacket and for some reason that made me sit down and cry. I cried because I missed Robert; I cried over Chris and all his misfortune; I cried over his little girl with Down's syndrome; I cried over my poor, struggling students, who worked long hours and tried to study and better themselves; and I cried over the wars in the Middle East and the poor state of the whole world. There was no bright spot.

The trip back was uneventful, and everything at home was as I left it. To keep busy, I did some housecleaning. My house is a tri-level model home with a pool, and I started with the upstairs master bedroom, dusting the nightstands and dressers, changing the bedsheets, vacuuming, and scrubbing down the master bathroom. Then I went down to the middle level and carefully dusted off my shiny black Kawai® grand piano that Robert had bought me as a house-warming gift after we bought the house. The coffee table in front of the fireplace received a good coat of wood cleaner before I did the country kitchen with a television set and a breakfast nook, spraying the marble-tiled kitchen floor and mopping it with a special cleaner.

Chris called that night as he had said, but we didn't talk for very long. He was busy with his job off the mountain, and I worked on profiling the suspects in Larry's murder case. Jule McCormick, the ex-nun turned psychology professor, who had found Larry's body in a pool of blood, had investigated Larry's background more. He had actually served in Iraq, as had, of course, the gay security guard downstairs in Larry's building. Both obviously had experienced killing in close combat. Ruth, the righteous, religious zealot who had buried two husbands and had a crush on Larry had come more to the forefront. And there must be reasons why Larry's roommate had suddenly picked up and left for Indiana. Was he fleeing a murder scene? What about the Chinese-American student who had grown up with Larry in Chinatown? And what about the Norwegian student, a big and husky woman who had been on trial for killing a gang member who had broken into her apartment? They were all possibilities, but I realized that I had to make their motives for murder stronger and do a better job of making them more believable.

I called my mother back on the farm in Wisconsin the next day, and promised I'd come out to visit her and my father, maybe at the beginning of August, but I didn't mention anything about Chris.

One day I called Susie and asked her to meet me for lunch. I told her I needed a reality check. She was teaching summer school, so I drove out to the college, and we had lasagna at an Italian restaurant nearby. I told her the whole story about Chris, his marriage, his institutionalized wife, and his daughter and asked her what she thought.

"He doesn't sound like a straight-up guy to me," she said. "But why take it so seriously? Have you slept with him?"

"Yes."

"Is he any good?"

"Yes, he's wonderful."

"Well, you know that the woman on the rebound seldom ends up with the guy."

"I know." I paused. "You're divorced and go out with guys all the time. Don't you want someone steady?"

"Maybe one day, but I like my life as it is right now. Why don't you have some fun with this Chris for now, and when you find out more about him and get to know him better, trust me, your feelings for him will cool off. You miss Robert still and you're vulnerable."

Level-headed Susie, always so practical.

CHAPTER ELEVEN

DATE WITH DR. FREDERIC PAGEL

After lunch, we returned to school. I went to my office to clean out some files and ran into Frederic Pagel, a global studies professor who had recently joined us from Pennsylvania. I had talked with him over coffee a couple of times and we had shared our experiences in Africa, where he had lived as well, and he knew that my husband had been killed in a plane crash over there. He was a brilliant man, distinguished-looking, tall, blonde, and blue-eyed with black-rimmed glasses, a true scholar who had received a grant or some kind of funding to go to Central Africa to work on carbon-offset trade agreements.

"Hi, Megan," he said as he literally bumped into me. "I'm sorry. I thought you were up in the mountains writing a book."

"I was, but I'm down in the flatland for a few days to reconnect with civilization."

"Time for a cup of coffee? I was just on my way out."

"Okay. Just give me a few minutes to lock up my office."

We walked over toward a small coffee shop near the campus.

"I heard you were going back to Africa," I said. "Congratulations on receiving the funding you applied for. When are you leaving?"

"Not until August."

"Are you excited?"

"Yes, of course. Working with companies to secure carbon rights to tropical rainforests is a major interest of mine. It's now become a multi-billion-dollar business." He paused and looked at me as if to check whether or not I was still interested.

"Tell me more," I said.

"There are four million acres of rainforest in Central Africa, and the local people get money every year they preserve it."

We entered the almost empty coffee shop and sat down in a booth by the window. A young waitress who looked like she might be a student took our order right away.

"What does your family think of all this?" I asked. "Aren't your parents medical doctors? They must be concerned about the situation out there."

"Yes, they both do medical research at Johns Hopkins in Baltimore, so they know a thing or two about tropical diseases, and they're trying to nix the whole deal. But I've been to Central Africa many times, and so have you, and you know that if you take precautions, get all the required vaccinations, and take malaria pills, you'll be fine."

"Well, I mostly stayed in North Africa, and as long as you didn't drink water from the tap, you were okay."

We sipped coffee, and he looked out the window for a few moments. "Do you like to go to the theater?" he asked out of the blue.

"I love it," I said. "Why?"

"There's a play by South African playwright Athol Fugard being performed at the Music Center in downtown Los Angeles right now," he said. "Do you know any of Fugard's works?"

"Yes, I've seen a couple of his most famous dramas."

"Care to go with me? We could go on Friday if you're free," he suggested. "I'll get the tickets."

"I'd like that very much." I paused and looked at him. "I'll drive then since I'm probably more familiar with the freeways. What's your address?"

He wrote it down on his business card and gave it to me. "It's right across from the campus," he said and gave me his cell phone number too. We agreed to leave his place at about six o'clock in case we ran into traffic.

"And I'll pay for the coffee," I said and asked the waitress for the bill.

"Thank you," he said, and then we went our separate ways.

Driving home, I tried to concentrate on the road. Going out with Fred seemed like a good idea to help keep Chris out of my mind for a while. Fred was a decent guy, but I already regretted accepting his invitation so quickly.

When Chris called that evening, I told him I'd been out to lunch with Susie and that I'd run into another colleague when I returned to my office. Since he'd lived in Africa too, we had decided to go see a play by a South African playwright on Friday. "I'll have my phone turned off, so if you call and I don't answer, you know where I am," I said.

"So, it's a he," he said quietly. "I realize I have no right to know who you go out with and where you go, but thanks for telling me anyway."

I was upset with myself that I'd let it slip that I was going out with a male colleague, but maybe it was for the best. Of course, he might decide to go out on a date too, but thinking about such an eventuality made me sick, and I didn't sleep well the next two nights.

On Friday, I started out early, before the rush traffic, so I could work in my office for a couple of hours. A little before six, I called Fred and asked if he could meet me at school, which he did. It had been a warm day as usual, but I had brought a wrap anyway as the temperatures drop in LA at night. Fred wore a dark blue sports coat over a white shirt and gray slacks.

The freeway traffic toward downtown was surprisingly light. Fred continued talking about the carbon trade; how Germany was onboard, but the United States was slow to sign on, which seemed to upset him. "If the local people want to cut down precious trees, we provide an alternative, and that's the part I want to be involved in. There's only one world, and we all live in it. There's only one economy, and we're part of it. Everything everybody does affects everybody else—with a few exceptions such as North Korea. Nationalism is a fading state in our global evolution." He sounded quite excited.

"And how are you going to enforce it? What's going to prevent the people from taking the money and cutting down the trees as well?"

"There's the village to enforce it. There's a lot at stake for the village here. And we use Google maps and can see when a tree has been cut down."

"You're an idealist," I said. "And it's all very interesting, but what you're describing is a utopian world, not a realistic one with overpopulation and wars over more and more scarce resources."

He didn't argue with me, and although I was interested in the topic, I realized I was tired and probably wouldn't be very good company that night.

I parked the car in the parking structure and, as I got out, Fred took my hand like a big brother would take his little sister's hand and guided me along toward the box office.

"How would you like to come out to Africa with me and be my assistant?" he asked. "I need someone who can write to help me with all the reports I have to submit. And you speak French too, don't you?"

I nodded. "That's an interesting idea," I said, and I meant it.

"I think we would make a great team," he continued.

"You're complimenting me," I said smilingly. "And it's true I miss Africa, but I'm already signed up to teach this fall."

"Well, I didn't mean right away," he said. "You could come out and visit me over winter break."

"That's very generous of you," I said and paused for a moment or two. "You're an extraordinary man, Fred, and what a fascinating business you're involved in! And you don't seem old enough to have had all this experience. How old are you actually?"

"I still have a couple of years to go before I turn forty."

"You're mature for your age."

"Thank you. What about my suggestion?"

"It's certainly something worth considering, but you have to give me some time to think it over."

"Of course."

The play was well done; but as soon as the lights went off, I was ready to fall asleep, and I started to dread the drive home.

During intermission and on our drive home, Fred talked about the important part Fugard had played in abolishing Apartheid in South Africa even though he was white; how he had been jailed and had his passport confiscated to prevent him from traveling abroad and spreading the word.

The traffic going out of downtown was horrendous. According to the radio, there had been two serious accidents somewhere on the grid, impacting the whole freeway system.

"Welcome to LA," I said as the traffic came to a stand-still.

"Do you want me to drive for a while?" Fred asked. "I can see you're tired."

"I'll be all right," I said, but it was after midnight by the time we arrived at his place, a small one-bedroom apartment that he rented furnished, he explained.

"I can offer you my couch if you don't want to drive home alone in the middle of the night," he suggested. "I would offer you my bed, but I don't have an extra set of clean sheets. I have pillows though and clean pillow covers."

I realized it was a smart thing to do, so I accepted. Fred was too polite and respectful to make any advances in my tired state. While I went to the bathroom, he made the couch ready and it was comfortable. I laid my head on the pillow and must have fallen asleep while he was still talking.

I woke up to the smell of coffee and sat up as Fred brought in two steaming cups. He had remembered to put milk in mine.

"You're spoiling me," I said.

"I try to treat my guests well," he said. "Sleep well?"

"Yes, great. Is this what I can look forward to in Africa?" I asked jokingly.

"Sure," he said and laughed. "I'm sorry I don't have any food in the house, so we'll have to go out for breakfast."

"Oh, coffee is wonderful," I said. "And I'd better get myself home."

"What are you doing this weekend?"

"I'm going to have to go up to my cabin and finish my book. I can't seem to think down here for some reason. It's always so noisy."

"Africa would be a good setting for a detective novel."

I agreed that it would. "And thanks for the invitation to come and visit you. I might just take you up on it."

"You're more than welcome."

I finished my coffee and got up. "Can I use your bathroom before I leave?"

"Of course. You know where it is."

"You're such a sweet man," I said as I returned and picked up my purse. I gave him a big hug, and he walked me down to my car.

On my way home, I was trying to think of Fred and Africa, but Chris's face would pop up in my mind. I was not very happy with myself, my feelings, and the mess I had stumbled into. Was what I felt for Chris real love? Could a permanent relationship be built on physical attraction alone? Did we have enough in common? Could a relationship with Fred grow into a happy one over time? Love was even more puzzling than a Rubik's Cube. It should not be a surprise that no one had been able to define it. Raymond Carver had made a pathetic attempt with his short story, *What We Talk about When We talk about Love,* in which four people sit around and talk about everything and nothing and then marvel at an old man who was depressed because his vision was obscured by bandages and he couldn't see his wife of many years. What phoniness!

CHAPTER TWELVE

A SURPRISE VISIT

A t lunchtime, I texted Chris and told him I was planning to go up to my cabin the next day, that I had a couple of broken sprinklers, and could he come over. He didn't call back right away as he usually did and it worried me. In fact, he hadn't called since I told him I was going out with Fred. Maybe he had decided to get drunk again. Maybe he'd found another one-night stand, as he had called it. I was getting paranoid. It was early evening when the phone rang, and I finally heard his voice.

"How was your date last night?" he asked in a matter-of-fact tone.

"It wasn't exactly a date," I said untruthfully.

"Are you going out with him again?"

"No, he's going to Central Africa to work on carbon-offset agreements. Do you know what it is?"

"I've read about it. Isn't it when we pay people in the jungle *not* to cut down trees?"

"Yes, that's how I understand it. This guy's a scholar, and he invited me to come along as his assistant and write reports for him."

"And are you going?"

"No, I'm signed up to teach this fall."

"Otherwise, you might have accepted the offer?"

"No."

"Why not?"

"I think you already know why. Can you come over tomorrow?"

"I'm down in Redlands right now, and I was actually thinking about driving over to see you at your place in LA tonight. Your address is...." He recited my address. "Am I right?"

"Yes, that's right. How did you know?"

"I looked it up?"

"But I'm not listed."

"Your name and address are listed as the owner of your cabin."

"Really? That's interesting."

"It'll take me an hour and a half, and I'll leave right about sunset. Do you have room for me to stay over?"

"Yes, another king-size bed that's going to waste," I said.

I kept busy tidying up and cleaning and was just as unsettled and excited as I had been when I was waiting for Robert to fly home from Africa with some sheikhs or potentates as passengers. Africa! How I missed it! But I knew subconsciously that I would not return there, at least not for now, although I was glad I had kept the option open.

It was too late when I realized that I should have gone out to buy some food; instead I called down to a trendy restaurant by the ocean and was told that they would be serving dinner until quite late.

It was after nine o'clock when I heard a car door slam, and I ran out to see if it was Chris. It was.

"Are you happy to see me?" he asked once again. He smiled, and although he had obviously not combed his hair and looked a little disheveled, he was a handsome devil.

"Yes, and you look tired."

He came in and put his stuff down before he embraced me.

"If you want to, you can put your bag upstairs in my bedroom and use the bathroom next to it," I suggested.

He followed my suggestion.

"It's been a long week," he said as he came downstairs again.

"How's the job going?"

"Good, but that's not what I meant."

I smiled and looked at him as if I weren't following his train of thought. "You must be hungry too," I said. "I didn't go shopping because I was planning to leave in the morning, but we have a good restaurant down by the ocean. I called, and they said they serve dinner until quite late. It's about a ten-minute drive."

As usual he checked his phone as I was talking.

"I didn't bring much in the way of clothes," he said.

"There's no dress code, although it's a bit pricey."

"That's okay; I have my credit card, and I'll grab my coat that I left in the car. You'd better drive because city driving is not my thing. Give me trees, hills, and mountains, and I don't get lost; but in the city I need maps, directions, and street signs. That's what I hated in New York. Everything looked the same. I didn't even bother to bring my car out there."

The parking lot was full, but I finally found a spot, and we walked into the elegant restaurant where several groups of people were still eating. If Chris looked a bit rougher than the rest of the crowd, I didn't notice. I was wearing a simple dress and my hair in a ponytail, although I had put on a pair of nice shoes at the last moment. These waiters, however —many of them older—were trained to avoid judging people and the content of their pocket books by their appearance.

"They sure know how to charge for wine here," Chris commented as he studied the wine chart, but he ordered a bottle anyway. "What's good to eat here?" he asked me.

"I really don't know. This is not one of my regular hangouts, but it was the only decent place I could think of that served food this late."

I remembered the last time I had been here with Robert when he too had commented on the wine prices. I declined the wine, but the older, formally dressed waiter poured a generous glass for Chris. We ordered chicken cordon bleu, and the waiter kept filling Chris's glass. When we finished, I asked for the bill. "I guess it's my turn to treat you this time," I said.

"Why? I'll pay with my card. You keep your money."

I couldn't help but notice that he left a 20-dollar bill as a tip, and I looked at him, probably with a question mark on my face.

"These people don't make very much," he said as we walked outside. "They depend on tips, a ridiculous system, but that's the way it is. This old guy may have a wife and kids. What do I have? And soon I'm probably gonna lose what little I have anyway."

"Well, I thought you had me."

He smiled and gave my ponytail a little tug. Then he put his arm around me as we walked back to the car.

I had to marvel at his generosity and his kindness. What was not straight-up with him? That he had waited so long to level with me, or 'lay the cards on the table' as he called it? Actually, I could understand it, although I wondered why divorcing a wife who had tried to kill him could be that difficult and take that long. Was it perhaps cheaper to keep this wife and pay for her expenses rather than divorce her and lose at least half of his assets?

At home again, he flung himself down on the couch. "I am really tired," he said. "But if I'm going to sleep in your king-size bed, where are you going to sleep?"

"In another bedroom downstairs, or maybe I'll crawl into the big bed next to you." I said and sat down beside him.

"You think you can sleep next to me and expect me not to touch you?'"

"Well, why couldn't you touch me?"

"Because you've led me to believe that we would just be friends until all my affairs are straightened out."

"I never said any such thing," I protested. "I'm a grown woman, and I've done a lot of thinking this week. We have only one life to live, and we have to make the most of it. So, what do you say to that?"

He stood up and pulled me up to him and engulfed me in his arms with a deep sigh. He kissed me, and I had just begun to return his kisses when he resolutely picked me up and carried me upstairs to my bedroom.

"I thought I heard you say that you were tired," I said, and put my arms around his neck.

"Not that tired," he replied as he laid me down on the big bed.

The next morning, I made coffee for us, and then I took him on a tour of the house. I showed him my office downstairs; the salt-water pool and deck with a view of the Pacific Ocean, but to my surprise he was mostly interested in the garage—which was actually a big mess. "I'm getting ready to sell the house," I apologized. "I can't take care of all this by myself."

"I know. And the memories are sometimes hard to get rid of too." He paused and measured the floor space.

"What are you doing?" I asked.

"Measuring."

"Yes, I can see that. But what for?"

"To see if a big car would fit in the space."

"What big car? I like my small Subaru. I don't want a bigger car."

"How would you like to have one of my classic cars stored in your garage?"

"What classic cars?"

"I thought I showed you my cars the day you came over. They were in the garage."

"I remember, but I don't know anything about cars, new or old, let alone classics."

"They're worth a lot of money."

"But you can't hide assets right before you get a divorce. If that becomes known, the judge will award your wife everything."

"I know. That's what my lawyer tells me, and I realize that I have to take care of my wife, as I told you, and I have no problem with that. But remember, she tried to kill me and there's a restraining order against her to stay away from me. And anyway, there's no way she'll be able to enjoy my money. It will all go to her sleazy father…and that is hard to take. The cars are not in the trust but are mine, and my lawyer said that I could probably get away with giving them away, preferably to a charity."

"So, I'm going to be your charity case?"

"Don't be silly. I have power of attorney for my wife and can sign for her, and so I should be able to transfer the pink slip to you."

"And what am I supposed to do with it? Maybe sell it, so that if I lose my job, I live off the proceeds for a year?"

"Oh, you could live for several years. They're worth about 300 grand each or even more."

"Wow! And you'll give one of them to me?"

"Well, other men give their girlfriends expensive diamond necklaces and other jewelry, so why can't I give you a car?"

"But I don't know if I want to be part of this scam?"

"It's not a scam. I'll only do it if my lawyer approves. It'll take several weeks."

"And where will I keep my car?"

"In the driveway. I'll get you a good cover."

"I guess it's my lot in life to have eccentric boyfriends–bush pilots in

Africa and affluent contractors who want to give me a 300-thousand-dollar car."

"I'm not affluent. Get that idea out of your head. I'm comfortable, but not affluent by a long shot."

"And what if I break up with you?"

"First of all, you won't break up with me. And second of all, I've dealt with all kinds of people for many years, and I know who I can trust and who I can't."

"And you think you can trust me?"

"Yes, no doubt about it. Cheating is not in your universe."

He was right, of course. Lying and cheating are not part of my vocabulary.

"We'll see," he continued. "Maybe a diamond necklace would be simpler."

"Well, I guess I could wear it to my book signings. That way people might think I actually make some money on these novels. In the meantime, we should probably go out and get something to eat. Then we can stop at the grocery store and pick up something to cook for supper here. We might even have time for a hike down to the ocean to see the sea lions, dolphins, and pelicans."

We picked up some chicken thighs and salad material, and after we'd put everything away, we walked down to the ocean, a half-hour hike. Chris was thrilled to see all the sea lions sunning themselves on the rocks in the surf. It's not a beach for swimming, so Chris rolled up his pants, and I had my new cropped stretch pants on, and we just waded barefoot in the cool water and looked at the tide-pools teaming with life—mostly crabs and sea urchins but also a few sea stars.

Back at the house, Chris looked at my piano. "Can you play something?"

"I don't play much anymore. I used to be an interim music teacher at an international school in North Africa. I got the job by default because I accompanied the Christmas program one year and the music teacher was leaving. The principal told me there were no applicants, so would I be interested in taking over. I agreed. My mother is an organist in her little church in Wisconsin. She majored in piano performance and helped me set up a program with really great textbooks with teachers' editions that told me in pretty good detail what to do."

"Play something."

"Okay." I sat down and played the beginning of "The Apartment" by Charles Williams, a jazzy and showy piece, but I stopped after a few minutes because I made too many mistakes.

"That's all I remember," I said.

"It's good. Play some more."

"I'm really hungry," I said. "Let's prepare some food for supper."

Chris fixed a chef's salad while I fried four chicken thighs. We took our time, and Chris decided to stay over one more night and left the next morning before 5:30 to beat the traffic and meet the guys at the job site in Redlands.

CHAPTER THIRTEEN

A LESSON IN CLASSIC CARS

C hris called in the evening and the next evening as well to say good night, and I told him I'd come up the next day, which I did. The following day he came over after he had checked on his local job sites. We drove over to his house to take Duchess for a stroll along the path that circled the lake. Duchess was, of course, excited and Chris let her loose to run and sniff on her own. On the way back, Chris pointed out a much bigger mansion than his, a monstrosity really.

"The owner used to be a competitor of ours for federal highway constructions," he said. "The house is huge, and it has an underground garage with turn-tables for over 20 cars."

"That's obscene," I exclaimed. "Quite frankly, I wouldn't want to live in a place like that. What's the point? You can only be in one room at a time. Even the queen of England lives in a relatively small, private section of Buckingham Palace."

"You're right. And it's going to be a hard one to sell eventually."

When we got back, Chris opened the garage doors to let the light in so that I could properly admire his old cars. "Which one do you like best?" he asked. "As I told you, this is the same car that Franklin D. Roosevelt used to drive." He pointed to the long, gleaming convertible. "Isn't it a beauty?"

"I'm sure it was a grand car in its day, but now you don't want to drive it because it's too valuable. I don't get it."

"It really does belong in a museum," he said. "I consider myself just a caretaker of the car until the next person buys it. This is a good climate for it in general though, and the garage is also insulated and climate-controlled for both summer and winter." He took a clean, white rag from a shelf and dusted off a few specks on the hood. "The leather can get dry and can crack, and the wheels have to be put in these cradles and lifted to prevent the tires from getting flat spots," he added. "So, which one do you want?"

"I don't know that I want any of them sitting in my garage, and I don't have climate control."

"We'll get a plastic bubble that can also be climate-controlled. We'll park the car inside and zip it up. What do you say?"

"I don't know what to say."

"Oh, come on. You're not going to say no to a three-hundred-thousand-dollar gift. You're not that jaded."

"You might be surprised," I said. "I like to have enough money too, but beyond that it seems to be a bother—as it is for you now because you've become so attached to it that you'll go to any length to keep it."

"I guess I don't have to worry that you love me for my money," he said and looked at me with his charming smile.

"You're right. I didn't know you had any more than I did until I saw your house."

"And, as I told you, the house really belongs to our family trust."

"And that is a relief to you, isn't it?"

"Yes, I guess it is," he said. He walked around the cars, seemingly to inspect them. "So, do you really want a diamond necklace instead?" he asked, but without waiting for an answer he added, "To tell you the truth, I don't think diamonds would suit you, so that's why I thought a car would be better."

"Oh, I guess I could make a diamond necklace work for me too," I said and looked at him coldly. "But you're right. I don't really like diamonds. Why do we insist on risking little African children's lives so that we can adorn ourselves with worthless stones? And they are worthless, you know," I added. "But they have been expertly marketed as a must-have for women—the marketing ploy of the century as it has been called."

"So, when I propose to you, I don't have to buy an expensive diamond ring?"

"Well, I wouldn't go as far as that," I said and laughed. "But seriously, why waste money on something worthless?"

"Oh, boy! I'm beginning to like you more and more. Yes, no doubt about it. You're the one for me."

"Listen, I want to tell you a story," I said. "A friend of mine knew a Jewish jeweler in New York whose wife always wore a huge diamond ring that everyone admired. But they thought she ought not to wear it as it might invite robbers. Well, the jeweler died, and the wife wanted to settle some of the estate. Her son asked if he could have the diamond ring. 'What diamond ring?' she asked. 'The one you always wear,' he answered. 'Oh, that. But that's not a real diamond. It's synthetic.' No one could tell, ...of course, ... no one would expect a jeweler's wife to wear a fake."

"So, you would be happy if I bought you a glittering fake from a department store?"

"Oh, stop it. Let's not go to extremes. But seriously, you don't have to buy me anything." I paused as I thought of another story:

"You know, once while we were living in Saudi Arabia, I got to know a local jeweler, a pawnbroker for the royal family who spoke only Arabic. Because I had studied Arabic, I liked to practice the language with this old guy, and we became friends—he called me his girlfriend. One day, as I was planning to travel back to the States, he asked me to take some pieces to New York and have them appraised. Among the pieces was an emerald ring, a large green stone set in a circle of diamonds pawned by one of the princesses who needed some cash quickly. These women were wealthy but didn't always have access to ready cash. My friend suspected that the emerald was synthetic because it was flawless; it was too perfect. I was more than happy to take the jewelry with me, and when I got to New York I took the ring and the other pieces to a big jewelry store in Manhattan, near the university where, by the way, you used to hang out. All the jewelry was genuine and worth thousands of dollars, but the emerald ring was fake; as my friend had suspected, and the only way the jeweler could tell was by removing the stone from the setting, placing it in water to measure its specific weight. There was no way to tell with the naked eye."

"You've sure been around in your young age, a real globetrotter," he said. "And you've become just as cynical as me, even though I've mostly associated with people around here. I guess people everywhere are a bunch of snobs. But I'd still like to salvage these cars if possible."

"But they're just things."

"I know, but they're beautiful, and there's nothing wrong with collecting and appreciating beautiful things—especially old things that really have a story to tell. We have to preserve some of our history."

"True. So, I guess I'll take President Roosevelt's car."

"Okay, so that's settled."

"When are you going down the hill again?" I asked as we walked back into the living room.

"Tomorrow morning. I'm staying here tonight, and you're staying here with me. I'll give you a key to the house, and then you can come and go whenever you want to use the gym, take Duchess for a walk, and play the piano. I'll call a piano tuner in San Bernardino to come and fix it up. You can probably see what needs to be done." He paused and walked over to the piano. I followed, and we examined the fine instrument more carefully. It appeared to be in good shape. I tried to play a couple of tunes from memory, and although it was out of tune, the strings and hammers were all intact.

"It actually needs several good tunings," I said. "One will not be enough, but it's a Steinway, of course, a top-of-the-line piano."

"That's good. As I told you it hasn't been played much since my mother died. Maybe you can teach me to play a little too. I would like to sit down and at least play some simple tunes. I took lessons for a while, but I don't remember anything."

Like a little kid, he sat down and played Chopsticks.

"That's a start," I said. "I'll get some music books for beginners, and then we can start lessons."

"Are you okay with walking home to your cabin tomorrow? I'm sure you can find your way. It's no more than a mile, but it is uphill. I may drive up again tomorrow night if you want to spend the day around here."

"Can you refresh me on how to use the machines in the gym?" I asked and walked over towards the work-out room, where we both worked out together. It was a lot of fun. Afterwards, we prepared a light supper from leftovers in the fridge and, since Chris had to be up early to go down the hill, we snuggled up in the big king-size bed early.

CHAPTER FOURTEEN

CHAMPAGNE FOR THE FISH

C indy came over one day just as I was thinking about going down to see her.

"I have to take a break from painting," she said. "And I figured you could take a break from writing." She'd taken her smock off and wore jeans and a blue T-shirt, and her cute freckled face didn't look a bit tired.

"Actually, I was just getting ready to go down to see you. Come on up on the deck, and I'll make some coffee."

"Great. Just a little milk in mine, please."

I went into the kitchen and made two steaming cups of Starbucks that I brought outside. "What are you doing on Saturday?" I asked. "It's the Fourth of July."

"I haven't planned anything yet. What do you have in mind?"

"Chris is having a little get-together with his brother and his wife and son and maybe his father and his father's significant other. Cheryl and Jonathan Day may be there too. You know them, don't you? Cheryl is Ed's wife's sister."

"Yes, I know them. Actually, Chad knows Jonathan quite well; they used to work together."

"Chris asked me to ask you if you and Chad would like to come. We'll have a barbecue on his deck, and then we'll take the boat out on the lake and watch the fireworks."

"That would be lovely." She paused as she took a sip of coffee. "And how are you and Chris getting along?"

"Too good to be true."

"Has he told you about all his trouble these past couple of years then?"

"Yes, and it's awful, but as I see it, it isn't his fault."

"No, it isn't. That wife of his was crazy from the start. Her whole family is despicable. Everyone said Chris was too good for her and warned him against her, but...of course...he was smitten by her sexy appearance."

"I told him that you said nice things about him, and I think it touched him, so now he may want to buy some of your paintings."

"See? He has good taste too. And, yes, any time. And I'll give him a good price. And how's your detective novel coming along?"

"Not at all. I went home for a week after Chris told me the whole truth. I talked to an old friend of mine that I've known since graduate school at UCLA. I needed a reality check and told her everything, and after she heard the whole story, she doubted that Chris was a straight up guy."

"I disagree. He's just had a string of bad luck caused by a crazy woman and some pretty poor choices he's made. After Robert died, you had a rough time too, so I thought you two would be perfect for each other."

"I hope you're right. As you can probably imagine, he's twisted my heart big time and sent my world spinning. He could hurt me tremendously if he wanted to."

"Why would he want to hurt you?"

"I don't know. Men and women hurt each other all the time," I said, but on a more cheerful note I asked, "And how's *your* work coming along?"

"Good. I have several paintings in a gallery in Hollywood. I'll have an exhibition there at the end of the month, and I want you to come."

"I'd like to."

"I have a few pastels in the small gallery down in the resort as well. As you know, we'll never get rich from our work, but that's all right, isn't it? Chad makes enough on his investments for both of us, and we've never regretted moving up here full time."

"Well, this country is all about investment and business, isn't it?" I said. "Artists and writers have it easier in Europe."

Cindy chuckled. "Yes, and so, you too, need a man who can make money."

"So true," I said, and we both laughed. I didn't mention anything about Chris's cars and his idea of giving me one of them in case it would compromise him, although Cindy would never divulge it to anyone if I asked her not to.

"When is the party on Saturday?" Cindy asked.

"Oh, I don't know exactly. Probably about 6 or 6:30 for the barbecue, and then we'll go out on the lake at about 8 or 8:30 or so. The fireworks start at 9:00 as I understand it."

"What do you want me to bring?"

"Nothing. I don't think we need to bring anything. Chris has bought champagne from a dealer he knows down in the flatland. I'm sure he'll grill steaks. That's his favorite. The guy is going to have a heart attack if he continues to eat so much red meat."

"How long have you been together now?"

"A little over a month, but it seems longer."

She finished her coffee and got up, ready to leave. "I'd better let you get back to work, and I should get back to my work too."

I walked her downstairs.

"See you Saturday," she said as she was leaving.

"Thanks for stopping by. I'll let you know if there's any change in the time. I look forward to seeing Chad again too." I added. I hadn't actually seen Cindy's husband since Robert died. Robert and I had been to their house several years ago. Now Chad would see me with another man.

I watched Cindy walk down the hill. She turned and waved. Although she was just a year or two older than I was, she seemed so much more mature. It seemed everyone was wiser and more mature than I was.

On Saturday morning, the idea came to me that I should make deviled eggs for the first time in my life. My grandmother and mother had always made them for our Fourth of July picnic back in Wisconsin. Carrying the plate of eggs in one hand and my black purse slung over the other shoulder, I hiked down to Chris's house early in the afternoon, looking all patriotic in a white T-shirt, a red blazer, blue stretch pants, and blue Toms. It was no use taking the car down as parking was tight around the lake on the Fourth of July. Many of the cabins were alive with people and decorated with red, white, and blue banners; and I thought about the year Robert and I had watched the fireworks from the deck of our own cabin, and how people had parked all the way up on our road and from there walked down to the lake.

An unfamiliar car was parked in the driveway, and I assumed it belonged to Chris's father. He, his girlfriend, and Chris were all out on the deck, so I went into the kitchen and put the eggs in the refrigerator. Chris must have seen or heard me because he came over to the fridge and gave me a big hug. "Honey, you're early and fresh as a red rose. Didn't Shakespeare say: 'My love is like a red rose'?"

"He might have, but you may be thinking of a poem by Robert Burns, a Scottish poet." Chris evidently had Shakespeare on his brain, and I made a mental note of borrowing some DVDs of Shakespeare's plays at the library and watching them with him sometime when we had more time, starting with Orson Wells in *Hamlet*. That should disabuse him of the notion that Shakespeare was boring.

"I would have come and picked you up, you know. Did you drive?"

"No, I walked."

"Good for you. I know you like to walk. Come out and meet my father and his girlfriend."

We went out on the deck to join them. "Megan, this is my father, Joe, and his girlfriend, Sandy." We exchanged greetings, and the usual conversation about my "exciting" life as a writer ensued. Joe looked a lot like his sons but walked with a cane.

"I have a new knee and a new hip, and I'm not quite steady yet," he said apologetically. His girlfriend was an attractive older woman in her sixties perhaps with discreetly colored brownish hair and a good figure. Both had red, white, and blue ribbons on their matching blue jackets.

"You look very patriotic today, Megan," Chris commented.

"I tried my best since it is the Fourth of July."

He was in his usual white tee-shirt and jean shorts, but he picked up a hat with an American flag in front and put it on. "This will have to do for me," he said and gave me another squeeze.

"So, I hear you have bewitched my son," Joe said jovially.

I laughed. "I think it's the other way around."

"Well, he's a handsome guy, isn't he?"

"And you're not a bit biased, I suppose," I said mockingly. "Actually, he looks a lot like his father, doesn't he?" I added and touched his arm to soften my previous sarcastic remark.

It was Joe's turn to smile and press my arm. He was, of course, a consummate salesman too and easy to connect with.

"Do you want to put up some decorations?" Chris asked me and handed me some red, white, and blue banners.

Ed and Elizabeth came shortly afterwards. Both sported red, white, and blue ribbons and baseball caps.

"Where's James?" I asked.

"He's with friends over at the resort. He and Thomas may bicycle over later," Elizabeth answered.

Ed's radio was crackling. "Sorry, but I have to have the radio on in case we have trouble," he explained.

No sooner had he finished his explanation than James and his best friend Thomas showed up. "Can we go swimming?" James asked, and Ed agreed it was okay, although it wasn't really that warm.

"I told Cindy to come at about 6 o'clock," I said as Chris was getting out the champagne.

"I know. I saw Cindy in town yesterday and told her to come earlier. They'll probably walk too."

"Yes, there are too many cars around today," I commented.

Cindy and Chad, who didn't have any children either, arrived shortly afterwards, and Chris poured the champagne. I hoped he wasn't going overboard with the alcohol as he had several bottles chilling in a cooler.

"And now let's toast to this great country of ours," Chris suggested, and we all took a sip. "And I also want to propose a toast to my amazing new girlfriend Megan, who now knows all my flaws and past mistakes but likes me anyway."

"Hear, hear." Everyone cheered.

"Let me propose a toast too then," I said trying to be cool. "To my friend Cindy, who brought Chris and me together." Everyone looked at Cindy and cheered some more, and except for Ed and me, they all finished their glasses. Chris poured more and opened another bottle.

"I didn't do anything," she protested.

I wasn't finished though. "And I want to propose a toast to Joe and Ed and their significant others for helping Chris recover from his recent ordeal." More "clinking" of plastic glasses and Chris poured more champagne. Then it was Joe's turn to propose a toast to Chris. "To Chris," he said simply, "for pulling himself out of a bad situation and going on with his life."

Jonathan and Chad seemed to have a lot to talk about. They were, of course, both businessmen and investors in the stock and bond markets.

It was time to fire up the grill. Elizabeth and I carried the dishes out on to the deck. Maria had been busy, I noticed, and we had food enough for an army.

"Who made the deviled eggs?" Joe wanted to know after we had started eating.

"I did," I said.

"That's what we always had back in Kansas on the Fourth of July," Joe said.

"I'm from Wisconsin," I told him, "and my grandmother and mother used to make them."

The boys had finally dried off and were sitting down over on the side by themselves, eating. They were, of course, waiting for the boat ride; but it was nearly sunset before we finished nibbling on the different dishes, clinking glasses, and cleaning up.

We finally moved down to the boat with blankets and more champagne. Evidently, we had to secure a place early. Ed made the flag that Chris had put in the back of the boat show off better with a small flood light next to it. Then he placed two big spotlights in front of the boat. He and the two boys took turns navigating into what they said was their usual spot. There were boats with lights and people everywhere. It looked as if the Spanish Armada was about to invade the resort. Many shouted greetings over to Ed, Joe, and Chris.

"What if there's an emergency, and you're needed?" I asked Ed.

"Then Chris will have to take us back in, but everything will be all right," he assured me. "We have good people in place."

"Is that why you put the extra lights in front?" I asked.

"Yes, but don't worry. Everything will be fine."

I sat down next to Chris, and he put his arm around me. "Are you cold?" he asked.

"No, I'm good."

He reached out for a soft blanket anyway and wrapped it around me. "Do you want more champagne?"

"No, thanks," I said. "As you can see, I don't drink that much. I actually prefer to drink soft drinks with the children."

He poured more for himself and the others. He drank his quickly and poured himself some more.

"Lay off the drink, man," Ed told him firmly, and I wanted to thank him but remained quiet.

"I'm okay, man," Chris countered. "It's just champagne, and Megan doesn't mind."

"As a matter of fact, I do." I said sternly. "And as I recall, we had an agreement about not drinking too much. If you give me your glass, I'll help you with it."

He passed the glass over to me. I took it and poured the champagne overboard.

"What are you doing?" Chris demanded.

"You saw me. I gave it to the fish," I said dryly.

"Do you know how much I paid for this?"

"A lot, I'm sure, but you can afford it."

He looked down and didn't argue. "I'm sorry. I didn't know it bothered you that much," he said, somewhat subdued and he sounded a bit annoyed. "I won't touch another drop," he said in a sarcastic tone.

"Good," I said and snuggled up to him, and as he tightened the blanket around me, I gave him a big hug and a kiss. He looked at me and smiled.

Both Ed and Joe glanced over at us. Ed nodded in approval, and Joe gave me the thumbs up. The father and two sons were obviously very close.

As the sky darkened, we could see people working on a big barge in front of us, and a few stray fireworks went off early. After dark, the real show started, and it was just as spectacular as any firework show down in Los Angeles. There were "oohs" and "aahs" from the crowd all around us.

"This is fabulous," I said. "Is it this good every year?"

"No, this is the best I've seen yet," Chris said. We sat in the back of the boat, behind the others. He had his arm around me and I leaned my head on his shoulder. I wished I could have made the moment last; but, of course, I knew that nothing lasts forever. Life is not a bed of roses. Or as

William Blake said, "Roses are planted where thorns grow." I didn't know at the time how many thorns I'd have to cut through to find the flowers.

After the twenty-minute show, Ed drove the boat in, and everyone got ready to leave. "Joe, you're going to spend the night here, right?" Chris asked his father.

"Yes, we'll sleep over."

"Good. I'll take Megan home. Don't wait up for me."

We all said goodbye. "Let's walk," I suggested to Chris. "It'll do us good after all the eating and drinking."

"Okay, as you wish," he replied, and we started out.

"What an amazing show!" I said. "Who pays for it all?"

"It's all private donations. Our company donates too. That's just how we do things up here."

"Do you want to stay the night?" I asked as we came closer to my cabin.

"I was waiting for you to ask," he said.

"Well, you told your father not to wait up for you, so I thought you planned to stay."

"You're pretty smart." He smiled at me.

"And I'm glad you didn't drink any more. I'll make it up to you."

"It'll be worth it then."

As soon as we got up to the second level, he picked me up and carried me to bed. Life was good.

We slept in Sunday morning, and it was almost noon when we walked back to Chris's place. Joe and Sandy were sitting out on the deck, and we spent the rest of the day with them. After lunch, we all walked along the lake trail at a slow pace. Joe was supposed to walk and steady himself on his cane, but he couldn't walk very fast yet. Duchess was full of excitement and sniffed everything.

Joe and Sandy left late in the afternoon, and that night I slept with Chris in his bed.

CHAPTER FIFTEEN

DELIVERY OF A STRANGE GIFT

C hris had already left when I woke up the next morning. He must have slipped out quietly because I didn't hear a thing. I fixed myself breakfast that I ate on the deck and enjoyed the solitude and beauty of the place before I took Duchess for a walk along the now familiar lake trail. When we came back, I worked out in the gym, and afterwards I went into the living room, which had only small windows and remained cool and dark even on a sunny day. It was a grand room, but it was not as cozy as my cabin, and I had the feeling that the ghost of a little child and her mother were leering from behind the walls. I played some scales and finger exercises on the piano, and when I opened the lid, the sound filled the whole room and made the ghosts go away.

A sound at the door startled me. It could not be Chris because he had said he was going down the hill. I stood up and stared at the door. It was just Maria.

"*Hola*, Miss Megan," she said cheerfully.

"Oh, hi, Maria. You startled me. I had forgotten that this is the time you come in."

"I can come back later if you want."

"No, come on in. I'm on my way out anyway." I closed the piano and got some of my things. "*Hasta luego*, Maria," I shouted into the kitchen.

"*Adios*," she answered, and I left. As soon as I walked into my own cabin, I put my things away and texted Chris, "I'm back at my place. Call me later."

I felt at ease; and in the afternoon, I sat down at the computer, and cranked out a couple of chapters. I wanted to finish the book in the next few weeks as school would start in six weeks, and I was trying to get in a trip to Wisconsin before that.

Chris called a little before sunset. "I've been really busy today," he said apologetically. "I got a piano tuner to come up on Thursday. Can you be over at my place by ten o'clock in the morning and tell him what to do?"

"Yes, that's fine, but I'm sure he knows what to do without me telling him."

"Well, I wouldn't know. But, in any case, it's better to have someone there."

"No problem. When are you coming up?"

"Do you miss me?" he asked.

"Of course."

"I'll stay with my dad tonight and come up tomorrow night. How's that?"

"Are you sure you can behave yourself without me?" I asked.

"Hey, what about you?"

"I'll manage, but don't let me wait too long," I countered.

"I'm trying to hook up with a guy who has an enclosed trailer that he hauls cars around in. He usually hauls cars from coast to coast, but for 350 dollars he'll haul the old Packard to your house. He said he didn't have any bookings this weekend. How about we go over to your house on Saturday, and you can help me handle it?"

"Oh, boy! I'm turning into one of your personal assistants, aren't I?"

"But I'm doing all this for you, but if you want to, we can make it another weekend. It's only that it takes days or weeks to book one of these trailers."

"You move pretty fast, don't you? I thought you said we wouldn't decide on the deal for a few weeks."

"Yeah, I know, but I want it over with. I want out of this ridiculous marriage. What do you say?"

"Okay. Have I ever said no to you?"

"No, you're a good girl."

"I'm spoiling you," I said. "But never mind. Call me tomorrow then when you have it all figured out."

"All right. I love you."

"I love you too."

He called the next afternoon to say he wouldn't be up until Wednesday, and late Wednesday afternoon he came up to my place with lasagna, a salad, and garlic bread from a restaurant down in Redlands.

"And where are we going to sleep tonight?" he asked.

"Well, we're already here," I said.

"I have to leave early in the morning, and you have to be at my place before ten to let the piano tuner in."

"I'll get up with you in the morning and go over and work out in your gym when you leave."

Before he left in the morning, we agreed that he should come back on Friday, and on Saturday I would leave for home and wait for the delivery of the strange gift.

The piano tuner came as promised and said he would tune the piano twice. He was a short man with bushy black hair and spoke so fast that it was hard to follow what he said. He had to tune the piano twice with a half-hour interval, he said, but I estimated that he would still have to come back in a couple of weeks' time. Since Chris had forgotten to give me money, I paid for the work. It was the first time I had paid for anything since we met, except for lunch with Susie and coffee with Dr. Fred.

I had meant to bring over some of my own music, but I hadn't had time to think about it, so I looked through Chris's mother's music in the corner music cabinet and found several sonatas by Beethoven and pieces by Schumann and Grieg, including a couple of my favorites: "Wedding Day at Troldhaugen" and "In the Hall of the Mountain King." What appropriate titles for this place! I wondered if these were Chris's mother's favorite pieces as well.

It was wonderful to play on such a fine piano, now that it was in tune, and I must have hammered away for hours because it was after two o'clock when I noticed that I was hungry. After lunch, I took Duchess for a walk, and it was evening before I went back to my own place.

I managed to work on my novel the next day before Chris came, and we went over to his place. Maria had left tamales in the fridge for us, and after we ate, I told Chris it was time for an evening concert. I opened up the lid again and it sounded as if I was playing in a concert hall. I played what I had practiced the day before while Chris was leaning back on the couch with half-closed eyes.

"Are you asleep?" I asked.

"No, I'm just enjoying the concert. My mother used to play, but she played more children's songs and Christmas music. I can't quite remember."

"Well, this must be her music," I said. "I found it in the music cabinet."

"It's possible. I can't remember."

"My mother is the organist in her small church back home, you know. And by the way, I'm going back to visit my parents for a few days the first week of August. It's hot and muggy out there now and lots of bugs, but I don't know when I'll have time in the fall."

"How many days?"

"Oh, maybe a short week."

"You mean a long week."

"I'll miss you too, but they're my parents. I'd like for you to come too, but you have work to do, and my parents are old-fashioned and wouldn't put us up in the same bedroom. And if they found out you were married, they'd be really concerned."

"I understand. I'll take you to the airport and pick you up when you come home."

No more was said about the trip at the time.

Two guys with a big truck pulling an enclosed trailer came early Saturday morning for the car.

"Do you want me to go home ahead of you?" I asked.

"No, we can both go in my car, and they can follow us. They have GPS in case we lose them."

We drove slowly down the hill and onto the freeway, where we stayed in one of the two rightmost lanes the entire way with all the other trucks and trailers. Since I didn't drive my own car, I didn't have the garage door opener, but I went around the side, and opened the side door—which was, fortunately, unlocked.

Chris drove the gleaming antique car out of the trailer and into my garage. Then he brought in four square boards and four jacks. "We'll jack it up a little to prevent flat-spots on the tires in case we don't have a chance to drive it for a while. We should try to drive it every few weeks though. It's actually better for a car like this to be driven once in a while than to be left in the garage for months on end."

I remembered that my next-door neighbor Ray was a car buff, and while Chris was busy with the jacks, I went over and rang Ray's doorbell since I saw his car parked in the driveway. Ray was actually a retired engineer and an inventor originally from the East Coast. He came over, and I introduced him to Chris. Then I texted Ken O'Brien, a young realtor I knew who was knowledgeable about old cars. He came over too, and we had a veritable car show in my garage. Chris brought out a six-pack of beer from a cooler in his car and passed the cans around. He was clearly enjoying being the center of everyone's attention. He certainly was a charming salesman, and I was halfway expecting the two men to sign up for a building project. On the other hand, the way he gulped down his beer bothered me.

"I thought the car had to be in a plastic bubble," I said as the two men left.

"We'll try without one first. The climate here should be mild enough and not too dry." He walked around the stately car, examining it closely to make sure everything was in order. "How about we go down to that restaurant you took me to last time I was here to celebrate," he suggested after finishing his inspection.

"Okay, but we have an agreement on how much to drink, right?"

"Don't worry, honey. I'm not an alcoholic."

"I know, but your drinking is starting to bother me. And all of a sudden I don't like the taste of alcohol anymore myself. I don't even like the taste of wine."

He looked at me curiously and his intense gaze was unnerving, and to escape it I turned away, as I usually did.

"Honey, is everything okay?"

"Yes, why shouldn't it be?"

"No reason. I'm just asking. Let's go and have a nice dinner, and I won't have anything to drink but water. How's that?"

"There's nothing wrong with a glass of wine, but drinking glass after glass is not good, and I'm starting to worry that you drink too much."

He came close and embraced me. "Tonight I feel like having water with my dinner."

"You're mocking me."

"Nope. I'm indulging you because I adore you. Do you want to drive?"

"Okay."

We parked way out and walked into the crowded restaurant. The same waiter was on duty, and he recognized us and took us to one of his free tables. I remember we had filet of sole with fizzy water, and Chris kept his word.

The next morning, he got up and wanted to make me breakfast in bed. What a guy! He appeared to be a hard worker. So, what if he had a glass too many? What was I worried about? No one is perfect. Life is about living in the moment, and at the moment all was well.

CHAPTER SIXTEEN

AN ODD QUESTION

We left my house the next afternoon, and Chris drove. "Do you want to go to your cabin or mine?" he asked.

"If you don't mind, I'd like to go to my place because I have my things there," I said.

The trip was uneventful, except for exceptionally heavy traffic on the 605 and the 210 freeways. We stopped at a little Mexican place in San Bernardino and had a taco each and more tacos to go for an evening snack.

He was gone by the time I got up the next morning—to my surprise, actually. He certainly was quiet in the mornings. I got up and made coffee, but it tasted bitter, and I drank only half a cup with some toast before I started writing. Fortunately, I had by now almost finished the novel and was working on revisions. Chris called in the evening and said he would be up on Wednesday because he had inspectors coming to sign off on different stages of the work at a couple of sites.

On Wednesday afternoon, I walked down to his place. Maria was there, and I texted Chris to tell him where I was before I took Duchess for a walk. When we returned, Chris was already home, and we put Duchess in her pen.

"I'll stay on the mountain for the rest of the week," he said. "There are more inspectors to pay off up here."

"What do these inspectors do anyway?" I asked.

"They're supposed to check that we follow the specifications on the drawings that have already been approved. The one we have up here now is honest I think, but the previous one was on the take. He just wanted the money and a little extra to look the other way."

"It's no wonder contractors have gotten such a bad rap. It's disgusting," I said.

"You've never seen our shop, have you?"

"No, where is it?"

"It's over on the highway. Let's go and have a look right now."

We drove up the hill to the main highway and through an open gate we entered a big yard behind a long, low building, where a big piece of machinery, an earth mover of some kind I assumed, was parked over on one side. Stacks of lumber and tiles of all kinds covered most of the space, and a big pile of gravel filled up the middle.

"This is a big operation," I said. "How do you keep people from coming in and stealing this stuff at night when no one's around?"

"Yep. It's a problem, and it happens sometimes. From sunrise to sunset there's always someone here."

"But there's no one here during the night then?" I asked.

"No, not really, and it's not a big problem. We lock the gate, of course, and have floodlights on all night. Most of the thefts are done by temporary workers who take a few pieces of lumber and other stuff, but word quickly goes around. Most of the guys I hire are recommended by other workers–often relatives."

A big truck with the bed built up by wooden slats drove in and parked by a pile of lumber. Chris went over and shook hands with the driver and his helper.

"Let's go into the office and say hello to Ana," he suggested when he returned.

Ana was a middle-aged Latina who looked very much like Maria but smaller and more alert. Chris introduced me and she spoke good English to me, but Chris spoke to her in fluent Spanish.

"Where did you learn to speak Spanish so well?" I asked. I had heard him say a few phrases to the guys who worked on my shed door, but this was the first time I heard him speak so native-like.

"I was brought up by a Mexican housekeeper, remember?"

"And she spoke only Spanish to you?"

"Yes, when there were only the two or three of us. My father wanted her to speak Spanish to Ed and me rather than broken English."

"Smart guy, that Joe!"

The phone rang and Ana answered very professionally in English. She had worked for the company over ten years and also did the billing, Chris said. She was evidently a loyal worker.

On the way home, we stopped at a fast food chain and ordered hamburgers to go. We ate on Chris's deck before we took a shower together, and Chris washed and blow-dried my hair. He seemed to be in need of some hair therapy again.

"Do you want a French braid or a fishtail?" he asked.

"French," I said, and he turned me around and went to work.

The braid felt a little crooked, but I gave him a good hug and thanked him.

The next day I went to the store to buy ingredients for lasagna that I made before Maria came so that she could do the clean-up. We had it for two days, and it was really good. On Saturday, I went to the library and checked out *Othello* with Lawrence Fishburne and Kenneth Branagh as they didn't have *Hamlet*. We watched it that evening on the big screen in Chris's upstairs sitting room.

"So, what do you think of Shakespeare now?" I asked as the credits came up.

"Pretty impressive."

"See what jealousy can lead to?"

"Are you saying I'm jealous?"

"Not at all. And that's good."

"Othello should never have listened to the gossip. He should have trusted Desdemona." He paused. "I know I can always trust you, can't I?"

"I hope so. And as you've already seen, I've decided to trust you too." I paused. "What was your favorite line in the play? Do you remember?" I asked.

"I remember the one about the old black ram tupping the white ewe."

"That figures. You *would* remember that one."

"I think we read *Othello* in the Shakespeare class I took a long time ago. Or at least we were supposed to read it, and the teacher, or maybe it was a student, pointed out that line. Maybe she thought we'd be more interested if we found out there was sex involved."

"You have a good memory," I complimented him.

"Sometimes," he said with a mischievous glint in his eyes. "And now, let's forget Shakespeare because in a moment I want to tup my own white ewe."

"Catch me if you can," I said playfully as I jumped up and ran behind the couch.

He was game and rushed after me as I scampered to the front, but then he just leaped over the couch and caught me by surprise. He quickly threw me down on the couch and held me there. There was no way to outsmart this man.

The next morning, after we'd made love again, I got up, grabbed my robe to go to the bathroom. Suddenly, I felt dizzy and had to lie down on the cool tile floor so that I wouldn't fall. Cold sweat broke out all over my body, and I lay still on my side, waiting for it to pass. After a few minutes, I tried to raise my head, but everything went black, and I lay down again. I didn't call Chris for help because I somehow knew it was just a momentary episode that would soon pass. Something similar had happened to me as a teenager back in high school after I'd taken a nasty fall. Everyone was concerned and wanted to haul me off to the hospital, but I had been back on my feet in less than five minutes.

After a while though, Chris came in. "Holy smoke! What happened?" he exclaimed as he saw me lying there stark naked, clutching my robe. He had put on his underwear and a tank top and right away kneeled down to feel my forehead and back. "Your face is as white as a sheet, and you're clammy all over. We'd better call an ambulance." He paused. "No, I'll take you to the emergency room myself."

"No, please, just leave me alone for a few minutes. I'll be fine. I just felt dizzy and lay down before I could fall. I've had this happen before."

"When?"

"Back in high school."

He took a wash cloth and let the water run until it was warm before he wrung it out and wiped my face, back, chest, and thighs. Then he took my pulse. "Does it hurt anywhere?"

"No. I feel better now. I'll get up."

"Let me get you some water first." He left me alone for a moment to find a glass.

"Thank you," I said as he held a glass of cold water up to my mouth. I sipped a little and felt better.

"I was too rough with you this morning," he said apologetically. "I don't think rough sex is for you."

"I don't think that had anything to do with it, and I feel better now."

He squatted down and picked me up as if he was a weightlifter and I was his barbell. Then he carried me into the bedroom and laid me on the bed. He built a pile of pillows for me to lean back on.

"I guess you've traded your little girl for a big girl to take care of," I said trying to be lighthearted.

"I'm not complaining; I love to take care of you, but I don't want to make you sick. I'll bring you something to eat."

"Thank you. Can you make me a boiled egg and some toast and maybe some tea?"

"Okay. Coming right up."

I raised my head and slowly got up to put on my robe and actually made it to the bathroom and back before Chris returned with a breakfast tray.

"Aren't you going to eat something?" I asked and gave him a piece of toast that he ate.

"You look a lot better. The color is back in your cheeks," he said. He took my hand and looked at me seriously. "Are you sure everything is okay?"

"Yes, I'm fine."

He remained silent for a few moments. "Have you had your period lately?" he asked out of the blue.

My jaw dropped. "What kind of a question is that?"

"Well?"

"That's a pretty personal question, isn't it? Even an impertinent one," I said irritably.

"I can't ask you a personal question after all we've been through the last few weeks? We've had sex almost every other day, and I haven't heard of a time when you've not been available...."

"Oh, my God! That's enough. This is too much. Are you keeping track of my menstrual cycle now too?" I paused. "It's often irregular when I come up to high altitudes."

"All right, but not this long. And I've also noticed that your breasts are firmer and fuller."

"Are you saying I'm getting fat?" I must have sounded pretty dense.

"Of course not. But are you sure you're not pregnant? I haven't seen any sign that you're taking any kind of birth control."

Actually, the thought of a possible pregnancy had crossed my mind briefly, almost subconsciously, but I hadn't dared let it come into my universe.

"I was married for eight years and didn't get pregnant," I said finally. I had been on the pill the first few years, but after I returned to the States, I had stopped taking them.

"Maybe your husband's boys couldn't swim so good," he said. "Maybe my boys are better swimmers."

"That's a funny metaphor."

"Metaphor or not, you should go see a doctor. I'll go with you if you want."

"Do you think it's possible?" I could barely hide my excitement. "I always thought it was my fault."

"People always think it's the woman's fault, but often it's not."

"How do you know all these things?"

"I've been through this before, remember. And I also looked it up."

"Oh, Chris, wouldn't it be wonderful? You're not annoyed with me, are you?"

"No, I'd love to have a baby with you. You'd be a wonderful mother. But it's too early to tell for sure."

"When do you think it happened?"

"I wouldn't be surprised if it happened that first time during the raging storm. You remember that day, I'm sure."

"How could I ever forget? Oh, Chris, I love everything about you, not just your pretty face."

He looked down and remained silent for a while.

"What's wrong? Can't I tell you I love you?"

"Yes, but as a child I was bullied with that phrase."

"Pretty face?"

"Yes. I thought it was something bad. I cried and didn't want to go to school. Ed had to take me and talk to the teacher. I didn't have a mother, remember?"

He looked up at me before he continued. "But it didn't stop, and it continued all the way up to high school. In high school, no one seemed to mention anything about it after I got laid by all the hot girls on campus, sluts really that I didn't care a damn about, but my status rose."

"That's ridiculous, and I'm so sorry. Children can be cruel, and I guess it's hard to grow up without a mother, even for a boy." I put my arms around his neck. "Do you want a boy or a girl?"

"It doesn't matter. But it's too early to get excited."

But I didn't want to listen. I couldn't help being excited. "Do you like children?" I asked.

"Yes, I do, but if we don't have any, it's fine too. There are too many people in this world as it is."

"That's true. A friend of mine, a reporter for a Los Angeles newspaper actually, was going out on an assignment to do a cute story on a mother who'd had quadruplets. When he got to her house, he learned that not only did she have quadruplets but she also had triplets with another man. She had taken fertility drugs both times even though she had two children before that. Her present live-in boyfriend was out of work—he was in construction actually—and so they were on welfare. My friend got really angry and wrote a nasty article about irresponsible behavior and also suggested that the doctor who had given her the fertility drugs should lose his license to practice medicine."

"Yes, not everyone needs to have children, but if we do, that's great because we can afford to take care of them."

"Let's take the boat out on the lake today. It's really warm," I suggested.

"It's too crowded today," he objected. "How about I take tomorrow off and we go out then? We can swim and water ski and have some fun."

"Then today, can we have dinner at Settlers Inn again? I feel like having some of that lobster bisque."

"I'll try to make a reservation, but it's hard to get a table there on such short notice."

He called his friend Al again, and…of course…he got us a table.

"We'll take my car," I proposed. "That way no one will know where you are. I'm beginning to figure out why you don't want to go out in public with me around here. You've probably bedded half the women in town."

"Now you're being ridiculous. The old floozies have either left or are fat and ugly with half a dozen kids."

I laughed and had never felt better. But then I remembered that I might be carrying the child of a married man. So much for Susie's advice to just have some fun with this guy.

CHAPTER SEVENTEEN

RESCUE ON THE LAKE

Monday morning was generally not my favorite day of the week as it was usually the beginning of a long work week, but this Monday was special—a whole day with Chris, swimming, perhaps water-skiing, and relaxing on the boat. I woke up before Chris and went into the kitchen to prepare breakfast and see what I could round up for our picnic lunch. Then I went out to say good morning to Duchess. Her dish was empty, but I knew Maria took care of feeding her just once a day, so I only gave her some fresh water. I heard Chris call my name and went back inside.

"Oh, honey, I thought you'd left. I must have had a nightmare," he said desperately.

"Why would I leave?"

"I don't know. I'm probably paranoid."

He came over and embraced me. "I guess I'm afraid of losing you."

Of course, he'd lost his mother and his little girl, and in the back of his mind he was probably always worried about losing anyone close to him. "Remember, I love you more than I'm willing to admit to myself," I said.

"Admit it," he said more cheerfully.

I just smiled in response. "Let's have breakfast on the deck. It's going to be a hot day, perfect for boating."

"Do you want to invite someone else to go out with us?"

"Not really, although we could invite James and his friend."

"I think James has a summer job at the gas station up on the highway. The owner is Iranian and probably wants to be on good terms with the sheriff."

We packed our lunch, put on our bathing suits, and slathered ourselves in sunscreen. I had often noticed how many people up here had brown, leathery skin from the sun and dry air.

"You try to maneuver the boat out this time," Chris suggested.

I was used to maneuvering boats around the lakes back home in Wisconsin, but Chris's boat looked different. "You show me how then."

I backed out of the dock carefully, put it in forward, and gave it some speed. There were already lots of boats on the lake.

"Slow down," Chris shouted. "It's not a race, and there's a lot of traffic. This is the tourist season, and many boaters are not experienced. We don't want to have an accident."

We coasted slowly around the lake once. "Do you want to try water-skiing first?" Chris asked and took a pair of skis and two orange life vests from the cushioned bench we had sat on last time we were out.

I strapped on the vest and jumped in the water. Chris threw the skis in after me and made sure the rope and handle were secure. It was a struggle to get the skis in place, but I managed and when I was ready, Chris gave the boat some gas and I was up in no time, skiing leisurely, trying to look cool, without doing any risky maneuvers such as jumping over the waves created by the boat, something I'd loved to do back in high school. At the other end of the lake, Chris turned as wide as he could, but I turned even wider and fell. Not cool! But I was quickly up again, and I skied back to our starting point. "You did great," Chris complimented me. Then it was his turn, and...of course...he did not fall. I was tempted to do a little zigzagging to challenge him but resisted. I would most likely have run into somebody and made a fool of myself.

"You're better than I am at whatever we do," I lamented.

"But I imagine you haven't done any water sports for a long time, and I'm on the lake every summer."

Just as we were about to anchor the boat and go for a swim, we spotted two boats collide not too far from us.

"Christ! What idiots!" Chris swore. "You don't go that close to other boats."

"Look," I said apprehensively. "A little child, a boy I think, fell in the water. The jolt from the collision must have knocked him overboard. It didn't look like he was wearing a life vest either, and no one is paying any attention. Drive closer."

The two boats were drifting away from us. "Man overboard," I shouted, but no one could hear me. I tore my life vest off, and as soon as I thought Chris was close enough, I dove in. The water was clear, but I couldn't see any sign of a child, so I surfaced.

Chris was pointing. "Over there," he shouted. "I see something over there."

I went down again and saw the little child, who was flailing his arms and legs but getting nowhere. I grabbed him and brought him up to the surface, but he fought me like a furious cat, and I had to slap his face to make him be still. Chris pulled the boat up close to us and hauled the little boy up and out of the water.

It all happened so fast that I had no time to think. As if by instinct, I had just been focused on saving the little boy's life. I took a deep breath and hoisted myself up and into the boat. "What's your name?" I asked as I wrapped a towel around him.

He didn't answer and started crying. He had probably been told not to talk to strangers. He was around three years old, scrawny and shivering from the cold water.

"Are your parents on that boat over there?" I asked and pointed to the boat.

"Yes, my mother and her boyfriend," he sobbed.

"They'll be back to fetch you in a short moment," I said and put my arm around him, trying to pacify him. "They just had a little accident with their boat crashing into another boat. We'll stay here and wait for them."

One of the boats finally did return. A hysterical woman in a bathing suit, her hair in wild disarray was screaming. "My little boy! Have you seen my little boy?"

"He's right here," Chris yelled back. "My fiancée rescued him; otherwise, he would have drowned. How can you let him in a boat without a life vest? He can't even swim."

The mother was not listening. She was relieved and just wanted her child. The boyfriend, tattooed up and down his arms, didn't even look at the kid.

"Whose boat is this anyway?" Chris yelled at the boyfriend.

"We're renting a cabin up here, and the boat came with it."

"Do you have license to drive this boat? Don't you know that you can't go so close to another boat?"

"And who are you?"

"It doesn't matter who I am, but my brother's the sheriff, and I'm about to call him and turn you in."

"Chill out, dude." The boyfriend tried to take a different tone.

"You idiot! You don't even realize that you almost killed a little child."

We were right next to their boat now, and I handed the boy over to the wailing mother. "Keep him wrapped up," I said. "You can keep the towel."

"Give her back the towel," the boyfriend snapped irritably.

"No, it's all right. You can keep it," I said. "It's all right." But she meekly unwrapped the boy and handed me the towel.

It was the last straw for Chris. "What a jerk!" he said loud enough for both of them to hear it. He took out his phone and called, keeping his eye on the other boat. "This is Chris Cronin. There's been an accident on the west side of the lake. The driver is unlicensed, and a child was thrown overboard without a life vest and almost drowned. He was rescued by my companion, and we're following the jerk back to his dock, or wherever he tries to go." He hung up.

"And you're going nowhere, buddy," he shouted to the boyfriend. "Except back to the dock where you came from; and I'll be following you." Then he turned to me as if he suddenly remembered that I was there too. "Sorry, honey," he said apologetically.

The boyfriend drove the boat back to the main marina, and Chris called the sheriff's station once more to let them know where we were.

We heard sirens, and I thought it was a little over the top as I hadn't quite processed what had happened and had to remind myself that we had just rescued a child from drowning, a little boy who by now would have been dead.

A young sheriff's deputy met us, and Chris pointed to the couple as he parked our boat a little farther out. Leaving me to fend for myself, he stepped up on the dock, shook hands with the deputy, and—fortunately— let the deputy handle the matter from there on. I followed to see if I could do something for the mother, and noticed Chris talking to a young preppy-looking man who looked like a local reporter because he was carrying a professional camera. They both came over, and Chris introduced me to Gary, an editor for the Mountain Gazette. Gary already knew my name and wanted a picture. My hair was, of course, a mess, but I smoothed it back the best I could. I called the mother and her son over, and we posed for photos. Then I told Gary, who seemed like a quick guy, the whole story. I was more than happy to put in a plug for my next book when he asked me what I was doing up here this summer.

The mother had calmed down and listened to my story. "Leave that boyfriend of yours if you want to see your little boy grow up," I whispered to her. I had the funny feeling that the boyfriend was none too happy to see the boy rescued. She and the boy joined the boyfriend, and they were all hauled off in the deputy's car.

As we were driving back out on the lake, I commented, "It's never a dull moment around here." And I added, "And if we ever have any kids, remind me never to get a divorce. I hope the mother breaks up with that jerk of a boyfriend. He didn't even look at the boy when I handed him over to the mother."

"I know, and you did a great job of rescuing the child, but I didn't see any gratitude. No thank yous."

"Never mind that. The mother was so hysterical that she couldn't think, and I didn't notice anything amiss. I was more afraid there was going to be a fight between you and the boyfriend."

"It wasn't worth it. Let the sheriff take care of it. That's what we pay him for, right?"

It was mid-afternoon before we finally had our sliced turkey-meat-and-cheese sandwiches with fizzy water and talked about what had just happened. The whole affair seemed so unreal, and it was going to take a while for me to digest it all. Chris gave me all the credit for the rescue; but, of course, without his guidance, I wouldn't have been able to find the little boy.

"I guess you didn't want your picture in the paper," I said.

"No, not right now. Gary knows that and respects it. He's a great guy and smart too."

We still went for a swim as if nothing had happened, but I was starting to realize how close we had been to seeing a child drown. After we dried off, I drove the boat back into the dock, where I parked and secured it without incident.

Ed came by in the evening to check that all was well and to hear the story first hand. He was in his uniform and announced his arrival with a small chirp of his siren.

"The deputy did a wonderful job of being on the spot quickly," I said.

"And you're all right?" Ed asked.

"Yes, and you'll read all about it in the local paper. The local reporter is a pretty sharp guy too."

Ed gave me a big hug when he left. "You're a brave woman," he said.

"Thank you, but as you can imagine, Chris took charge of the whole situation. I wouldn't have been able to be of any help without him. I think we make a good team."

"I know you do," Ed said with a nod of approval.

Chris just stood there smiling proudly. Praise from Ed obviously meant a great deal to him. We walked Ed to his black and white police car.

CHAPTER EIGHTEEN

A TRIP TO WISCONSIN

C hris went back to work on Tuesday, and I went back to my cabin to work on my novel. It was now almost ready to be sent off to the editor. I needed it off my hands before school, and the publisher wanted it in good time before Christmas, which is the ideal time to release commercial books, so the pressure was on.

At lunchtime on Thursday, Chris came over with a copy of the weekly newspaper with my picture and story on the front page. It was well written and accurate as I suspected. The quality of some of these regional, small-town papers was surprisingly high; although this one, as Chris has said, was heavy on crime reporting.

After Chris left, I went down to Cindy's to show her the picture and tell her the story first hand. The more I told it, I realized, the more I got it out of my head, although I still had moments when I shuddered to think what might have happened to the little boy.

Cindy had, of course, already heard all about it. They really didn't need a newspaper in this town. She offered me a glass of ice water, and we talked about life in a small town before she showed me her latest paintings; which were truly beautiful, especially the pastels, and most especially a pastel of the small island in the lake that Chris and I had swum to the day when I had discovered his big scar. "I need to buy that picture from you, Cindy," I said. "That island has some special meaning to me. In fact, maybe Chris and I can buy it for each other for Christmas or our birthday. We have the same birthday, you know."

"Really? I didn't know that. What a funny coincidence!"

"Yes, but we were born one year apart. He's exactly one year older than I am."

"Well, I thought you were about the same age. So, everything is working out between you then?"

I agreed.

She looked at her picture of the small, idyllic island. "I have to include it in my upcoming show, but I'll write 'sold' on it," she said. "You'll have to wait until Christmas though before you can take it home with you."

"That's fine," I said as I finished my coffee and got ready to leave. "I'll be on my way then. See you soon."

On Friday morning I called my mother and told her that I was planning to come home on the following Wednesday, unless they had anything else planned. They didn't, so I ordered a return ticket to Milwaukee via Chicago online with return to LAX the next Tuesday.

"You're leaving me alone for a whole weekend?" Chris complained when I called him that evening.

"Well, it's time for your boys to take a break from swimming," I said, jokingly, following up on his metaphor.

He chuckled. "What are you going to tell your parents?"

"You mean about us?"

"Yeah. You've got to tell them something, don't you?"

"I'll tell them that I have a new man in my life now. How's that?"

"I'll take you to the airport," he offered.

"No, that's too far for you to drive. I have to go home a couple of days early to pack and buy presents for everyone, especially my two little nieces. I'll take the shuttle. It's very convenient. But how about picking me up the following Tuesday, when I come back?"

"Sure, but I'll be glad to take you too."

"I know, but the shuttle is fine."

It was a hot weekend, and we spent Sunday swimming off the dock, as the lake was crowded with boats and probably unlicensed operators, and Chris was reluctant to risk taking his boat out. In the evening, Chris set up the FaceTime App on our iPhones, and I promised to call him from Wisconsin.

I felt sad after saying good-bye before he left for work late Monday morning; and I wondered why on earth I had decided to go back to Wisconsin when everything was going so well here, but it was too late to think about that now. I went back to my cabin, mechanically picked up some clothes and toiletries, and drove home. I texted Chris as soon as I arrived and then called Mom to see if she or Dad could pick me up in Milwaukee or if I should rent a car. Chris called later on in the evening on FaceTime, and we talked about everything and nothing until the battery ran out on my phone. He called again the next evening as well, but I didn't text him again until I was sitting at the gate at LAX waiting to board: *All well. I'm ready to board at LAX. Don't call as I have to put my phone in airplane mode. Will text you when I arrive in Chicago and then when I'm home on the farm. I love you.*

I wished the week would go fast, and that I would soon be getting off the return flight and that Chris would be here to pick me up.

In Chicago, I barely had time to run to the other gate from which the connecting flight to Milwaukee departed, and I had no time to text Chris or call my mom.

The airport in Milwaukee is small compared to LAX. You don't see much security either, and both Mom and Dad were in the baggage area near the gate to meet me. A big woman, my mother sported a new permanent but wore the same flowered dress I'd seen her in for years. My father's hair looked a litter whiter, but he still had a lot of hair for his age.

"I saw your old suitcase and knew you'd made it," my mother said after we'd given each other big hugs. "How was the trip?"

"The same old hassle. Flying isn't what it used to be."

Never a loquacious man, my father just picked up my suitcase, and we walked to their big black car. "Oh, so this is your new Lincoln Town Car," I said. "It looks nice, but it must be a gas guzzler."

"We don't drive that much," my father answered.

Driving north through the familiar countryside brought on feelings of nostalgia. The farm houses were few and far between out here, and there was hardly any traffic. My mother talked about their neighbors and people at church, and I talked about school and my book.

When we turned off the main highway, I spotted an Amish family in their horse-drawn carriage. "So, the Amish are still around, I see," I commented. "It's amazing to see them still in their traditional garb. It must be hot. It reminds me of the Middle East, but somehow I don't object to the Amish women's bonnets and long dresses the same way as I object to the burqas and veils that women have to wear over there." I thought about it for a moment. "Maybe it's because the Amish men also wear traditional clothing, while the Muslim men can wear whatever they like," I continued. *Showing off good-looking buns in their tight designer jeans*, I wanted to add, but held my tongue. My mother wouldn't have appreciated it.

"The Amish are peaceful people," my father said. "They work hard, pay their bills, and don't bother anyone. The people over in Arabia fight all the time and hate our way of life. They kill people that they don't like and those who don't think like them, even their own. Mohammedanism is a sorry excuse for a religion in my view."

"People say Islam now, Dad, and most of the Muslims are peaceful," I said.

"Then they're welcome here," my father continued. "But we have too many of them out here in Wisconsin that are not peaceful, and they've caused a lot of trouble."

"Are you still working on your PhD?" my mother asked. She didn't like to talk about politics.

"No, not really. My teaching and writing take up most of my time. I'm almost ready to send my fifth novel to the publisher. And there's a new man in my life now."

"Oh? Who's that?"

"His name is Chris Cronin, and he's a year older than I am, but we have the same birthday. We were both born on the 17th of September. Isn't that funny?"

"Cronin. That sounds Irish. Is he Catholic?" My mother wondered.

"I haven't asked him, but he's not very religious."

"What does he do?"

"He's a contractor."

"What kind of a contractor? A carpenter?" She didn't sound pleased.

"It doesn't matter, Mom. He's a nice guy, and he runs his family's contracting business, which his father started; and, by the way, his father is from Kansas City, a good old Midwesterner."

"Don't you meet any doctors or professors out there?"

"Don't be such a snob, Mom. And anyway, the young doctors in

California nowadays you wouldn't like anyway. They're either Asian or women. They're good doctors, but they're not tall, handsome, blue-eyed men with beautiful wives who spend their time doing charity work." I sighed because I realized then that I would never fit into this conservative society any more, and it saddened me. My parents were good people as were most of their neighbors and friends, but they were still stuck in the past back here.

"I know, dear. I just want the best for you."

"Chris is very smart, and he has a college degree. He's also very handsome, and I love him," I said irritably.

"Looks don't last, dear. How long have you known him?"

"A couple of months. Actually, I should text him to let him know that I've arrived safely. On Saturday, we'll call him on FaceTime, and you can talk to him and see his face."

The big old white farmhouse, the barn, and the outbuildings came into view on the right side, and as we drove into the driveway, good old Biscuit, a white and brown sheepdog, came running along his long leash line to greet me, jumping up to lick my face as soon as I opened the door. The heat and humidity were palpable, and I pushed him down to get my suitcase to go inside to safety and air conditioning—to Biscuit's disappointment.

The cluttered, built-in porch, filled with raincoats, rain boots, and bug spray, led into the spacious country kitchen and living room that looked the same as before, with the same furniture my grandparents had left when my father took over the farm. Nothing much changed out here.

I quickly texted Chris, while my mother set the table for a supper of fried chicken and homemade potato salad. After we had finished eating and had cleaned up, I sat down at the old Story and Clark piano, a work horse of an instrument, popular out on the prairie since the 1800s. I played some finger exercises while my mother searched the music cabinet for our usual pieces for four hands. As we always did when I came home, we began our concert with *March Millitaire* by Schubert, a piece we'd had a lot of fun with when I was growing up.

"Oh, I forgot to tell you; Chris has a beautiful Steinway grand piano at his house. We just had it tuned, and it sounds gorgeous."

"Does he play then?"

"No, I think his mother did. She died of breast cancer when Chris was eight years old."

"I'm sorry."

"Oh, it's a long time ago. He has an older brother who's actually the town sheriff. Their father never remarried, but they had a housekeeper who's still with them. They live in the resort town where Robert and I bought our cabin."

"I see." She didn't show too much enthusiasm.

On Thursday, my brother George and his wife Joyce came over for lunch with my two nieces Hannah and Lauren, and I passed out presents for everyone. For the girls, I had two toy computers that actually worked, and both girls soon figured out how to use them and sat completely absorbed the whole time they were there. I wondered if I had started a bad trend.

Chris called late that night. He wasn't thinking of the two-hour time change, and I was already in bed.

"Now don't go around trying to fix broken sprinklers for lonely women back there," I said jokingly. "And remember our agreement."

"What agreement?"

"Our alcohol-in-moderation agreement."

"Oh, honey, do you think I have time for anything but work right now? I'm trying to drive the guys this week, so I can take some time off when you come back."

"That's a great idea!"

"And while I'm here working my butt off, you're probably out gallivanting with your old boyfriends."

"I haven't seen any of them, and I probably wouldn't recognize them anyway. Everyone around here is so overweight and out of shape. It's the muggy heat, I think. You can't move around much out here." I paused. "Oh, by the way, on Saturday, do you have time for FaceTime, so you can talk to and see my parents?"

"What time?"

"Well, eight o'clock here is six o'clock in California. Is that too early?"

"No, I'll be ready for you. Do you want me to call?"

"Yes, that would be good since we don't really have any set plans other than getting ready for Sunday—when my aunts, uncles, cousins, and their kids will come over for Sunday dinner."

On Friday, we all went to town and saw the old familiar shop keepers who knew from the weekly announcements in the local newspaper that I was home for a visit. Many said they'd bought my books, but I doubted they had read any of them.

Chris called on FaceTime after supper on Saturday as promised, and although his face was distorted on the screen, as I'm sure mine was, it was fun to see him.

"Mom, come and say 'hello' to Chris."

"Hello, Chris," she said as I held my phone up so Chris could see her face.

"Hello, Ma'am," he said politely and then to me, "Megan, you didn't tell me your mother's name."

"Karen," I said. "Karen Viets."

"Hi, Karen. You have a lovely daughter, and thank you for sharing her with me. You're done a good job of raising her. She has completely bewitched me."

"Thank you, Chris."

"I hear it's hot and humid back there. Why don't you come out here for a visit? I have lots of room for you to stay, and my house is right on the lake."

"We'd like to someday," my mother answered hesitantly.

"Chris, are you home?" I asked.

"Yes."

"Show my mother your grand piano."

He held his phone up to the keyboard with the name Steinway right above it, and my mother was duly impressed.

"Show her your grand fireplace too."

He did, but when I asked him to go outside and show his house, he balked. "Megan, no, I'm sure your parents have just as nice a house."

I went over to my dad. "And this is my dad, George Senior."

"Hello, Sir. How are you?"

"I'm fine, thank you. Nice to meet you. I hope you're treating my daughter right."

"I try my best. I hope she's not complaining."

"Dad, don't embarrass me. I'm a grown woman and can take care of myself." Then to Chris: "We're having a big family reunion tomorrow. This is all the stuff we've prepared." I showed him all the dishes that were still cooling on the counter.

Everyone said good-bye, and Chris called back on the regular phone. "How did I do?" he asked.

"Good. You're a big talker anyway, so it's not difficult to get a conversation going with you."

In the morning, my mother and I went to church, where my mother played the organ as usual, while my father stayed home. He was not particularly fond of church people. At the family reunion in the afternoon, we counted twenty-seven people in total, and it was wonderful to see everyone, good to reconnect with my roots. I missed having family in California. Chris had his father and brother close, but I hadn't heard of any uncles, aunts, or cousins anywhere. Maybe Chris and I would have children, and they would at least have a grandfather, an uncle, aunt, and cousin close by. The Latinos often had large extended families, and even though they sometimes didn't have much in the way of material things, they always seemed so happy. The ubiquitous, hard-working gardeners drove around in their little pick-up trucks, rakes and spades sticking up from the truck beds. They were never alone. There were always two or three crammed into the front seat, playing their Mexican music, singing or whistling along while sipping their cold drinks and generally hooting it up.

Joyce, my sister-in-law, a tall and capable woman that I had known since childhood, had brought an ice cream maker and was making ice cream outside in the yard, despite the heat and chiggers. Dad had inflated an above-ground swimming pool that he was still filling up with cold water, while the smaller children were splashing around in it, squealing for joy. Biscuit was running back and forth on his leash line in great excitement. Truly, Norman Rockwell would have had a field day with the entire scene.

After the women had packed leftovers to take home and helped clean the place up, I called Chris and told him all about it. "And how was your day?" I asked.

"Long. Duchess and I walked over to your place and sat on your deck for a while. Then I went around and checked on the job sites. I miss you."

"I miss you too. I'll text you when I'm at the gate in Milwaukee and give you the flight numbers and arrival time. It will be over six hours before I arrive at LAX if you still want to come and pick me up."

"I'll follow your flight on my phone and either be at the gate or in the baggage area."

It was with a sense of melancholy that I packed the next afternoon. I was just getting used to being home when it was time to leave. My feelings for Chris may have cooled a little bit. My mother was right. I should take my time and not rush headlong into the first relationship I'd had since Robert was killed. But what if I was pregnant? It was a little late to back out then.

CHAPTER NINETEEN

BACK IN LOS ANGELES

C hris was at the gate when I arrived at LAX. I was one of the last ones to get off, and I saw him leaning against the back of a chair, looking at his phone. He had donned one of his many sports coats for the occasion, and I had to stop to catch my breath before I walked up to him and said, "Hello, Chris."

"Hi, honey," he said with a big smile. "I was just about to text you to see if you'd missed the flight."

"Sorry, I sat in the back of the plane," I said.

He put his phone away and embraced me. "I missed you. How was the trip?"

"It was fine. You could have picked me up at the curb, you know."

"Well, I had plenty of time."

I tried to pull myself away, but he wouldn't let me go right away. "We'd better get my suitcase before someone else picks it up and carries it away," I said finally. "How did you get all the way up here? How did you get through security?"

"Oh, I have my ways."

He took my hand in his and picked up my carry-on with his other hand. His hand felt warm and strong and surprisingly soft. I gave it a little squeeze, and looked up at him, but he was intent on reading the signs up above. We didn't talk much as we walked over to the escalator and down along the concourse to the baggage area, where I quickly spotted my old bag.

"Your suitcase doesn't exactly look like it belongs to a world traveler," he said and laughed.

"Well, it has been battered around a bit. In some of the Third World countries I've been to, baggage is tossed around mercilessly, but this is an old Samsonite® and Samsonite® used to be the Cadillac® of suitcases and this one will last a few more years."

He evidently didn't believe in rolling luggage and resolutely picked it up and carried it. Maybe he thought that pulling a suitcase on wheels was unmanly. I took care of my carry-on, and we walked hand-in-hand in between a myriad of people, cars, and vans to the parking lot. As usual, it was a hassle to get out of there, and I kept quiet so he could focus on the traffic.

"You seem distant," he said as we drove along Pacific Coast Highway to my house.

"I'm sorry. I guess I'm tired, and it was a little sad leaving my parents. After all these years, they still seem to enjoy each other's company. I wonder what will happen to us. How will you feel about me when I'm old and fat?"

"And how will you feel about me when I'm gray and wrinkled?"

"You'll probably age gracefully like your father."

"Anyway, I don't love you for your looks. I've learned my lesson when it comes to hot women."

"So, are you saying I'm not hot?"

"Are you trying to pick a fight? You're very hot. As you may have noticed, I can't keep my hands off you."

We drove in silence for a while. "The weather is sure great here compared to back home," I said.

"Yes, it's especially pleasant here along the coast." He paused. "Is everything okay with you? Is everything the same as when you left?"

"Do you mean, has my period returned?"

"Well, I didn't want to be too personal again."

"Nothing has changed, and I made an appointment to see the doctor on Thursday at one o'clock. I tried to make the appointment on Wednesday, so you could come with me, but he wasn't in on Wednesday, the receptionist said."

"That's okay. I can stay one more day and go with you. Afterwards, we can drive together up to my place."

"Yes, we could do that."

We were soon at my house, and Chris parked in the driveway next to my Subaru and got the luggage.

"I guess we should have a key made for you," I said. "And you should have a key to my cabin too."

"Yeah, if you give me yours, I'll take care of it," he suggested.

I unlocked the front door and walked inside ahead of him.

"Where do you want me to put your bags?" he asked as he came in behind me.

"Upstairs would be good. I need to run to the bathroom first," I said as I kicked off my shoes. He took his boots off as well.

I followed him up the stairs and flung myself on the bed. "I'm exhausted," I said. "I have to take off my bra; it's killing me."

He took off his jacket, put it on a chair, and sat down next to me. "Are you leading me on?" he asked.

"No, I'm just uncomfortable, that's all." I sat up, wiggled out of my bra under my loose blouse. Then I touched his chest. "How's your scar?"

"The same. It will always be there, I guess. Do you want to check it out?" He removed his skimpy tank-top, put it at the foot of the bed, and leaned back on my decorative pillows.

"It looks a little better," I said untruthfully because it looked pretty much the same. "The mental scar this episode left you with will probably take longer to heal."

He remained silent.

I don't know what came over me. Maybe it was because I'd just come from home, had seen family members, and reminisced about our childhood antics, but I felt playful all of a sudden and remembered a little nursery rhyme my old Norwegian grandmother used to recite when I had scraped my knees or elbows. Mimicking my grandmother, I kissed Chris's scar, blew on it three times and recited the rhyme in broken Norwegian: "Legga po lammelort...."

"What's this? Voodoo medicine?"

"This is how my grandmother would make my 'owies' feel better," I said and unbuckled his belt and unbuttoned his pants so I could see the scar in its entirety. I decided to give it another kiss. Then I lay my hand on his bulging crotch.

"You *are* leading me on, you little vixen," he said, but he didn't move. Maybe he was waiting to see if I had more tricks up my sleeve; which, of course, I didn't.

"Vixen?" I said. I was reminded of a fable that I sometimes told my students to illustrate how small-minded people confuse quality with quantity. "Do you know that my students don't know what a vixen is?"

"Well, they probably grew up in the city and never saw a female fox."

"My students always want to know how long an essay should be. One of our business teachers regularly requires a thirty-page research paper on some uninteresting topic, and many students complain, so I tell them the story about the vixen and the lioness. Do you remember it?"

"No, I don't think so."

"Well, a vixen with several cubs sneered at a lioness because she had only one cub. But the lioness stuck up her nose and replied proudly, 'Only one, but a lion.' In other words, some people confuse quality with quantity. I love that story."

Chris looked at me and smiled indulgently, and I pulled him toward me. He pushed me over and pinned me down to the bed hard, covering my face with kisses. I couldn't move an inch, and all of a sudden I felt claustrophobic.

"If I told you to let me go, would you stop?" I asked as I took a deep breath and tried to remain calm.

He immediately loosened his grip. "What's this? Do you think I would hold you down against your will?"

"No, and I don't want you to let go completely. It was just a hypothetical question. Your strength scares me sometimes. It makes me feel helpless," I tried to explain.

"Are you playing some kind of game with me?"

"No, I just read about a rape case in the *Chicago Tribune* on the plane coming back. Actually, I didn't finish it because it was just too horrible, and it made me think of one of my students. I remember that her name was Joyce because it was the same name as my sister-in-law. She was a good-looking black girl from the inner city, and she came to my office one day in a mess. She said she had been gang-raped by her ex-boyfriend and two of his friends who had come to her apartment one night when she was in her nightie, a skimpy baby doll dress, she said. She let them in and they took turns with her—pinning her down and raping her." I paused. "She kept blaming herself, that she shouldn't have let them in when she was in her skimpy pajamas, but I kept assuring her that it was not her fault. 'You could have been in your birthday suit,' I told her, 'and it still wouldn't be your fault. They have committed a crime, and we need to report it to the police and turn them in.' But she was ashamed and wouldn't do it. We have counselors at school, but at that time we didn't have any female counselors, so she came to me. I called a woman psychologist who had taught some classes for us, and she took it from there. But Joyce didn't return to school, and I was thinking how awful it would be to be pinned down against your will by some ugly guy and not be able to free yourself. The claustrophobia, helplessness, and the humiliation you'd feel."

"Guys who do that should have their dicks cut off," Chris interjected.

"But it's not always as simple as that, is it? What if the girl lied?"

"Honey, do we have to talk about such terrible things now? I'm trying to make love to you. Let's focus on something more positive."

"Do you think rape is a sex crime?" I persisted.

"No, I think it's classified as just a crime. Can we talk about something else, like how to be good to your loving partner? Or don't you want to do it now? We can stop if you wish. Maybe you're hungry."

"I'm actually very hungry, but it can wait till afterwards."

And so, I tried my best to forget about Joyce and the woman in the newspaper, so I could concentrate on being good to Chris. But he was actually much gentler with me after that conversation.

Wednesday was warm and sunny, and we spent the whole day at the beach. We packed a lunch early, brought a picnic table, umbrella, chairs, and towels and set up camp near a lifeguard station after Chris had read the bulletin with information on the water temperature, high and low tides, and checked with the lifeguard about rip tides.

I told him that what he was doing was a good idea and more people should check with the lifeguard before they went swimming.

"That's what we always did at the beach house we rented in Malibu."

"How many summers did you spend there?"

"I don't remember. Maybe two or three, because Ed got summer jobs, so we had to stay home." He paused and was seemingly trying to think back on those days. "Ed and I both had friends come and stay too. Maria was there part of the time with one or two of her kids, I think. And my father would come on weekends, and other times too, with one of his girlfriends. He wasn't celibate, you know, after my mother died, but thank God, he never remarried. I would have hated having a stepmother and living with one of those girlfriends permanently."

"Sandy seems like a good woman."

"Yes, they've been together for several years now."

We ran into the waves, ducked under them, and swam some distance back and forth parallel to the coastline outside the breakers. Then we body-surfed like a couple of children until our fingers looked like prunes. We had a late lunch and took naps after we had laid our towels on the warm sand. I was thinking of the doctor's visit the following day and looked forward to it and dreaded it at the same time.

"What do you think the doctor is going to say tomorrow?" I asked as Chris took my hand in his.

"I'm sure he's gonna say you're pregnant. How do you feel about that?"

"Good, although if I'm not, it will be fine too. I'd actually like to have some time together before we have kids. And then there's my work. But, of course, there's never a perfect time for children, is there?"

When we came home, we rinsed off and went swimming in the pool. Later we ate odds and ends in the refrigerator, and then it was time for bed.

CHAPTER TWENTY

A VISIT TO THE DOCTOR

B ecause of the difference in time, I woke up before dawn the next day. Chris was still fast asleep, and I walked outside, filled up the pool and checked the landscaping, which was minimal. It would be awkward to tell my supervisor at school why I needed a leave in the spring. I would have to say I was engaged and planning to get married. He was an old-fashioned, elderly man. *Why was Chris stalling when it came to getting a divorce?* I wondered. *Was it because it would cost him too much money? Would he rather carry on the way we were so he wouldn't have to pay off his wife?*

The students wouldn't notice. They were pretty self-absorbed and had their own problems. Susie would smile indulgently, knowing I wasn't as street-smart and world-wise as she was, but she wouldn't really care. If I took a leave of absence, I would have time to concoct another mystery plot and would persuade Chris to come to the opera, concerts, and other shows with me. I estimated the baby would be due around March first.

I heard Chris stir, but I didn't go up to the bedroom to see him right away. Instead, I made coffee and toast and served him breakfast in bed.

"How come you got up so early?" he wanted to know.

"It's almost ten o'clock in Wisconsin, remember? And I'm anxious to get going."

The doctor's office had only three other patients before us—a highly pregnant woman, a young girl, and an elderly woman—when we arrived for our appointment. The pregnant woman looked bored. It was probably not her first one. She was huge, and her baby must be due any day now, I thought. If I was up in the mountains with Chris when I was due, I suddenly realized, I wouldn't have my regular doctor on hand to deliver the baby,

Chris observed the weigh-in, waited while I provided my urine sample, and listened with interest to the questions posed by the nurse as she took my blood pressure. She placed a stool by my head as I lay down on the examination bed, so that he could hold my hand during the pelvic exam. He was certainly playing the part of a concerned husband.

The doctor came in and shook our hands. He was a little older than I was, and I had known him for a long time.

"Yes, there's a baby in there," he said. "Seven or eight weeks looks about right, and everything is normal."

"I'm a little old to have my first one, aren't I?" I said.

"No, not at all. Many women marry later today, and you're in excellent health."

"That's good to hear."

"And how does the husband feel about this?" he asked Chris.

"Great. And sex is okay for now, right?"

Was that what was foremost on his mind? Why did he always have to be so blunt?

"Yes," the doctor answered. "Up until the seventh month or so. I'll let you know. Make an appointment to see me again in six weeks, earlier if something changes, or if there's any bleeding or blotching. I'll write a prescription for some multivitamins." He looked at Chris as we got up to leave. Chris thanked him, and they shook hands as if the two of them were co-conspirators in this affair.

"So, now it's official," I said as we left. "How do you really feel about it?"

"Oh, honey, I'm happy." He put his arm around me and gave me a reassuring hug. "And I really have you in my clutches now, don't I?" He smiled mischievously, but the fact that I was in his clutches worried me for a moment before I realized that he was also in my clutches.

"And you know, we don't have all the time in the world to wait anyway," he continued.

"I think it's going to be a boy," I said. "What do you want to call him?"

"Honey, it's too early to get excited about it."

"I know, but I can't help it. And it's so ironic. I tried to get pregnant the last couple of years when my husband and I were married. Now I'm not married and pregnant. Life is truly puzzling." I paused. "So, what names do you like? Chris junior?"

"No."

"Joe?"

"No, something more modern, like Kevin or Jeffrey or Michael. But there's plenty of time to decide. And maybe we shouldn't tell anyone quite yet."

"It's going to be hard for me to keep quiet. I wonder what they'll say at school."

"Don't tell them."

"I won't for a while, not until I apply for a leave of absence around Midterm."

"You could get a job a little closer to me, you know."

"Yes, that's a possibility. Or I could take you up on your offer and finish my PhD."

"Now, that's the best idea I've heard yet."

We stopped at Norms for lunch before we went home to pack up a few things for the mountains. Chris spent most of the time in the garage, checking and polishing the old car.

"If we're going up in one car, I won't have transportation up there, and you'll have to take me down again in a few days," I said. "I have to prepare for school."

"You can use my car. I'll drive the truck. You don't want to take a break from school and stay with me then?"

"No, but I may have to take a leave of absence in the spring if you're sure it's all right,"

"Honey, you won't ever have to work if you don't want to. I can take care of both of us. You know that."

"Yes, but I'd rather work. I don't think being a stay-at-home mom is for me right now. Maybe someday, and besides, you have another wife to take care of."

"Not for long. I talked to my lawyer while you were gone, and my father-in-law has put another obstacle in the works, but she says it won't hold. I know this is a sore spot for you, but by the end of the year it will all be over, I promise."

Little did he know that his prophesy would come true, but not in the way he expected it.

CHAPTER TWENTY-ONE

A REMINDER OF THE PAST

W e stopped in Redlands so Chris could check on his work sites, while I read the newspaper in the car.

"I'll show you a small apartment building we own while we're here," he said when he returned.

It was a well-maintained eight or ten-unit building with manicured landscaping and relatively new cars parked in front.

"One unit is empty and being renovated," he said. "Let's go in and take a look."

It was freshly painted in light beige with white trim and new beige carpeting. "It looks attractive," I said. "I could live here and be closer to my school and to you too, and I wouldn't have to drive up and down the mountain road every day."

"Don't be silly, but it's a nice place. And we have two other buildings over in San Bernardino. Joe takes care of them, and he doesn't tolerate deadbeats. If he sees a tenant throw trash on the ground, even if it's not directly on the property, he tells them he won't renew their lease."

When we got up the hill, he checked on his other work sites too, but I decided to sit in the car.

"I called Maria to leave us something in the fridge," he said when he returned. "When I come to think about it, we'll have to tell Maria. She'll be hurt if we wait too long. She'll be happy for us."

On the way home, we stopped at the grocery store up on the highway to pick up some greens and something to drink. Chris preferred this store to the one in the resort, he said, maybe because he knew everyone who worked in the resort, and I was probably an inconvenience that had to be explained away.

As we were looking for salad material, a woman with bottle-blond hair came up to Chris. "Hello Chris," she said. "So, what are you doing out buying your own groceries?"

She wore heavy make-up, a short skirt that barely covered her butt, and knee-high black boots. She was attractive, but she was certainly a woman who'd been around the block a few times.

Chris glanced at her and then at me. His face reddened, and he looked flustered as if he didn't quite know how to deal with both of us at the same time.

"I see you need a haircut again," she said. Her voice sounded raspy.

He brushed back his hair with his hand. "No, it's all right," he said irritably. "I had it cut down in Redlands a couple of weeks ago."

"Well, are you going to introduce us?" she said and looked at me.

"Megan, this is Maddie," Chris said as he tried to regain his take-charge composure. "She works in a beauty salon."

She didn't seem to pay attention and was looking the other way. She finally turned to me. "Sorry, honey, I didn't catch your name?"

"Megan," I said acidly. "And I'm a teacher."

"And she writes mystery novels," Chris added, but she didn't seem very interested.

"I'm up here to see my parents again," she said to Chris. "I'll come over for a drink one evening." She smiled at him flirtatiously and left.

There was no need for me to ask who she really was. I knew from both Chris's and her demeanor that she was part of Chris's past, but it annoyed me how familiar she was with Chris, inviting herself over in such a matter-of-fact tone. We drove back to the house in silence.

On Saturday afternoon, while Chris was at work, I had planned to take Duchess for a long walk but got sidetracked by the piano again. In the early evening I heard someone at the door, and when I went to check, the woman from the grocery store had entered without knocking or ringing the doorbell. She had on the same skirt and boots, and could have looked pretty, but with her platinum hair and caked-on make-up she looked like a hooker.

"Can I help you?" I said coldly.

"Where's Chris?"

"He's not here at the moment. He's at one of his job sites." I went closer and smelled alcohol.

"I'll just wait." She walked right past me and sat down on the couch. "Do you have anything to drink, honey?"

"No, and it may be a while before Chris comes home," I said.

"And who are you again, honey? The girlfriend of the week?"

"I'm a good friend, yes, and what do you want with Chris?"

"That's none of your business, is it?" she said without looking my way.

"Oh, yes, it is," I replied dryly. Blood rose to my cheeks; my face was getting hot, and I could feel my annoyance growing into anger. "If you think you can come here and intimidate me, you're sorely mistaken. Please leave right now. I'm taking his dog for a walk, and I can't leave you here by yourself." I was trying hard to stay calm. "If you give me your phone number, I'll tell Chris you came by, and he can call you if he wants to."

"Oh, honey, he has my number."

"Chris and I have a date tonight, and I don't particularly want to drag along one of his drunken old floozies," I said sarcastically. "And if you don't leave this minute, I'm calling the sheriff."

She broke into an ugly laugh and glared at me. "Oh, I know Ed too, honey." She got up and walked toward the bathroom. "I need to use the bathroom."

I called Chris and told him one of his old girlfriends was here. "The one we met in the grocery store," I said. "She's ugly, and she's been drinking."

"If she won't leave, let her stay until I get there. I'll take care of it."

"I was planning to take Duchess for a walk and go up to my cabin. Do you want me to leave her here alone?" I said in disbelief.

"Yes, if you can't get rid of her."

"Why don't you meet me at my cabin, and then we can take care of it together?"

"That sounds like a good idea."

But as soon as I'd said that, I regretted it. He would, of course, come here first anyway, and God knows what he'd promise her.

I took my time getting ready. The floozy had gone into the bedroom and was lying on the bed on top of the covers—boots and all. I left her there and took Duchess with me, walking slowly up the hill and, sure enough, I saw Chris turn off the road and head down to his place, while Duchess and I continued up to my cabin.

It was almost an hour before Chris drove up my driveway.

"So, you went to see her first," I said accusingly, as if I was talking to one of my students that I'd caught cheating.

"Yes, you have a problem with that?"

His sharp tone surprised me. "As a matter of fact, I do have a problem with that. What did she want from you?"

"Money."

"Money?" I said in disbelief. "And you gave it to her?"

"Yes, I went down to the ATM and withdrew some cash, and it took a while."

"Oh, my God. How many of these exes am I going to have to deal with?"

"None. I'll deal with them."

"Do you give them all money?"

"No, but sometimes. What's wrong with helping someone out?"

"I don't know, but it's odd," I said. "That's not what people in a committed relationship do." I paused, but he didn't answer, and I continued: "Wouldn't you think it odd if one of my old boyfriends came barging into my house half-drunk while you were there by yourself, insulting you before going into my bedroom and plunging himself down on my bed?"

"I'd throw the bastard out," he said.

"That's what I tried to do, but she wouldn't move."

"Okay, I get your point."

"I wonder if you have some kind of White Knight syndrome," I said.

"What's that?"

"A guy with a White Knight syndrome, according to psychologists, feels the need to take care of women in distress. It's a condition that can lead to abuse."

"I've never abused a woman."

"No, in this case it's the other way around. These women could abuse you. I've read cases where the women have gotten houses and cars out of men like that."

"That's not gonna happen. And you talk like there's an army of them out there." He stood there for a moment looking at me sadly. "There's been only one other woman I've given money to and that was one of Amanda's classmates, who came over a few times after Amanda was committed, and I helped her out with some money for her kids."

"Didn't she have a husband?"

"No, I don't think she married any of the dudes she slept around with."

"Do you give money to men too?"

"Yes, I do take care of my men if they need a few dollars when they're out of work."

"And what is this Maddie to you anyway?" I asked. "I'm sure she wanted more than money from you."

"She may have wanted someone to drink with. We dated in high school. She was quite pretty then and one of the hot girls. I'm sure you've already figured out that I had an inferiority complex, and I thought she'd raise my status. I really never cared for her, or any of the others either for that matter."

He certainly laid it all out on the table, but he wasn't finished.

"While I was away in New York, she married a guy from the San Fernando Valley and moved out there with him. She got divorced about the time Emily died. Her parents still live up here, and whenever she'd drive up to visit them, she'd come over, and we'd get drunk together."

And have rough sex together, I thought. *I imagined she'd be good at that*. But I didn't say anything.

He came over to embrace me.

"No," I said. "I need some space right now. I can't deal with all of this." I covered my face with my hands.

"If you think I would jeopardize our relationship and spend the night with her instead of with you, you're insulting me." He sounded hurt. "The only thing she did for me was save me from drinking alone sometimes. And, no, we didn't sleep together, or if we did, I was too drunk to remember. I know I've done things in the past that I'm not proud of. After the trial and with both Amanda and Emily gone, I guess I was lonely. But that's all over now."

My heart was beginning to soften, and I uncovered my face and looked at him.

"I love to be with you," he continued. "Do you think I could go on nature hikes with a woman like Maddie? She wouldn't know a squirrel from a skunk. Or do you think I could take her out on the lake with James, Ed, and Elizabeth?"

I walked over to him and put my arm through his. "Okay, I think I understand," I said. "Everyone has a past. Let's forget it, rewind the tape, and start all over." I smiled up at him. "Where shall we spend the night? Your place or mine?"

"Mine, if you don't mind. Maria has left food for us in the fridge, and Duchess is better off in her own pen. Come on, Duchess."

Duchess was happy to go out again, and after we had eaten some of Maria's Mexican casserole, we put Duchess on the leash and took her for another walk. It was good to be back at Chris's beautiful house, but the incident with Maddie had unsettled me, and it took me a while to get her out of my mind.

Later that night, we went upstairs and watched television, more news about inner-city protests and violence.

"If they'd just get out of these projects," I said. "I substituted in Los Angeles for a couple of months, and if the school I was assigned to was located near a project, I knew what kind of day I was going to have."

"They seem to be breeding grounds for crime," Chris commented. "I feel sorry for the unappreciated police who have to go in there. And now we have some overgrown thugs held up as role models." He paused before he continued, "And why do they build these projects in downtown areas anyway? Build them out in the desert on the California-Arizona border. Irrigate some land, so they can grow some crops."

"But that might mean more segregation," I said.

"How can they be more segregated than they already are?"

"Actually, this could be a good project for you," I said. "Design a village and build it. That's what they did in Saudi Arabia. I remember exploring the desert with a new map one weekend. We wanted to drive out to a town that was marked on the map—I can't remember the name—but we had never heard of it or of anyone who had actually seen it. We followed directions and drove along a state-of-the-art highway, which all of a sudden just ended. Where the town was supposed to be, we saw only a pile of carefully stacked rocks. The map had been printed prematurely, and the town was just in its planning stages." I looked at him and he seemed interested. "Coordinating the required people and permits and building a new town would be a worthy project for someone with your special talent," I said. "And I could help with fund raising and PR."

We laughed at our lofty plan, but I tucked it away in the back of my head. I could at least use it as the setting for my next novel.

On Monday morning, I drove Chris's car back to my cabin and worked steadily to polish my book. I reread it and spellchecked it once more, merged files, and printed out a back-up copy before I attached it to an e-mail and sent it off to the publisher. Late Saturday afternoon, Chris came over, and on Sunday we took the boat out just far enough for some good swimming. The lake was too crowded farther out, and it was too hot for a hike, although we did take Duchess for a walk in the evening.

CHAPTER TWENTY-TWO

GETTING READY FOR SCHOOL

The next week I started planning for school. I roughed out course calendars for the semester, but I had the templates for my syllabi on my computer at school; so midweek I drove home to get my office keys and my parking sticker before I drove over to the college, where I uploaded PowerPoint presentations from last term to my new courses. Then I made folders, and still had plenty of time to visit with colleagues before all the meetings started.

"Did you finish your book in the midst of all your romantic escapades in the mountains?" Susie wanted to know.

"Yes, it's off my hands, sent off to the publisher in good time before the deadline. Fortunately, Chris has had a lot of work now too; otherwise, I wouldn't have gotten anything done."

"So, who dun it this time?"

"I'm not going to tell you. You'll have to read the book when it comes out."

"Oh, come on. Give me a hint."

"What have you been up to since I saw you last?"

"Oh, the usual. Ashley and I went to Washington, DC for a few days after she came back from her dad's. You know, she's twelve now, and it's time for her to get a little cultured."

I nodded in agreement before Susie continued: "Then she went to camp for two weeks while I developed new course materials."

"I may stop teaching for a while and finish my PhD soon," I told her. "Chris said I could be his kept woman for a while. What do you think about that?"

"Go for it, girl. I wish I had a sugar daddy too."

"He's not my sugar daddy."

"Whatever. Who cares?"

I was tempted to tell her everything, but I held my tongue. Maybe later.

"Oh, by the way, *Carmen* is on at the Music Center," Susie said. "Did you know that?"

"Yes, I saw the reviews. Do you want to go?"

"Yes, let's."

"How about taking Ashley, and then I can invite Chris."

"Can you get him to come?"

"I think so. Actually, it will be my treat. I'll get tickets for all of us."

"Are you sure? The tickets are expensive."

"I know, but I haven't spent any money all summer. Chris pays for everything. The only thing I've paid for is the piano tuner. Did I tell you, Chris has a beautiful Steinway piano? You have to come up and play it sometime."

"I will. But you have to invite me, you know."

"Is there a matinee performance on Sunday?" I asked.

"Yes, I think it's at three o'clock."

"I'll call and get the tickets. Do you want us to pick you and Ashley up on Sunday about noon? We'll be coming down from the mountains, and it will be more or less on our way. Or do you want to be independent and drive your own car?"

"No, that would be awesome."

"Then we could have lunch before the show."

After laying out all I needed for my first classes on Monday, I drove my own car up to the mountains for the weekend. I went straight to Chris's place and looked through his mother's music to see if I could find anything from *Carmen*. And, yes, she had the Toreador Song, which I practiced a few times before I texted Chris and took Duchess for a walk.

Chris came shortly afterwards.

"Guess where we're going on Sunday afternoon?" I said.

"I have no idea." He sounded tired.

"To the opera. I have already bought tickets. Say yes, please."

"Okay, but I probably won't understand a thing."

"Oh, you will. It's *Carmen* by George Bizet, the most accessible opera there is. You'll love the story, and you've heard some of the music. Actually, I found the most famous song, the Toreador Song, in your mother's music cabinet. Let me play it for you." I played and sang the few words I remembered.

"Bravo," Chris called out. "And, yes, I have heard that song."

"The story is about Don José, who is engaged to the lovely Micaéla, but is seduced by the gypsy girl Carmen. He's completely smitten, but Carmen soon tires of him and goes on to seduce a famous bull fighter. Don José is beside himself with rage, and we'll see how he handles the situation."

"Oh, that sounds really dramatic. I imagine he kills somebody." His tone was sarcastic.

"We'll see, and I think you'll actually like it. Later we'll see *Aida* by Verdi and *La Bohème* by Puccini, and then you'll know your ABC's of opera: *Aida, Bohème*, and *Carmen*, get it?"

I called Susie before we left to tell her we'd be a little late.

"Do you want me to drive?" Chris asked. We had to take my car, of course, because his Range Rover was parked in my driveway at home.

"That's okay," I said. "I'll drive since you drive so much all week, and I know where we're going. You can drive home if you like." I looked at him all dressed up in a beige, collared golf shirt, with a sports jacket over dark brown slacks. "You look nice," I said. "I don't think I've ever seen you so dressed up before."

"Yeah, take a good look. You won't see it very often."

"Actually, it'll be a great experience for you to go someplace where you don't have to take charge, as you always do. You'll be completely incognito! And you'll have to listen to two smart women if you want to learn something," I said teasingly. "Do you know that Susie and I met in New York once when I was living overseas to see Richard Wagner's massive Ring Cycle, which is an opera based on Norse mythology? That's when we both had husbands."

"You and I should go to New York sometime," he suggested.

"I thought you didn't like New York."

"That's right, but it will be different if I go with you and don't have to hang out with some immature punks."

We picked up Susie and Ashley a little after noon.

"How are your piano lessons coming along, Ashley?" I asked.

"Good."

"What are you playing?"

"*Für Elise.*"

"The whole thing?"

"No, only the first part."

"She's working on the second part now," Susie added.

We arrived downtown in the middle of the lunch crowd, but Chris got us a great table at the Pinot Grill with a view of Grand Avenue. He may have bribed the hostess for all I know, or dazzled her with his glittering eyes. He usually got his way.

"I was just telling Chris about the time we went to New York just to see the Ring Cycle," I said to Susie. "Remember?"

"How could I forget? We're a couple of crazy women, Chris."

"I'm sorry, but I'm not with you on that one. I don't know much about music." He turned to Ashley. "How do you like opera, Ashley?" He may have been hoping for an ally.

"It's all right," she answered.

"Good girl. I took piano lessons once too, but I don't remember much. My mother used to play for me."

"Maybe my mom could teach you again," Ashley suggested.

"Do you think she'd want to?"

"Mom, can you?" she asked her mother.

"Yes, but Megan can teach him too."

Ashley didn't say any more. She ordered a hamburger and the rest of us the special: grilled salmon with mixed vegetables. Chris asked for the bill.

"I should treat you since you got the tickets, Megan," Susie suggested, but Chris paid no attention to her.

On our way to the box office, we passed a souvenir store.

"Oh, Mom, they have fancy duct tape. Can I have one? I'm completely out," Ashley pleaded with her mother.

"Duct tape?" Chris said surprised. "What on earth does a little girl do with duct tape?"

"Make stuff."

"I'm sure I have a case of it in my office."

"But these have pretty patterns."

"Will you make something for me if I buy you some? That is, if it's all right with your mom."

Susie looked at me, and I just shrugged my shoulders.

"How many do you want?" Chris asked.

Ashley looked at her mom. "Three," she said to Chris.

Chris looked at the price. "That's a lot more than I pay for my duct tape."

"It's the latest craze for girls right now," Susie explained. "They used to have it only at arts and crafts stores, but I see entrepreneurs everywhere have jumped on the bandwagon." She turned to Ashley. "Now you have to hold on to it during the performance."

"We still have time to put it back in the car if you want to," Chris suggested. "Come on, Ashley. Your mother and Megan can talk opera while we're gone."

"He's cute, isn't he?" Susie said as we watched them walk down to the underground parking garage.

"Yes. It's not so easy for me to just have some fun with him for a while, as you suggested. And anyway, it's too late for that now."

"What do you mean?"

"Nothing." I bit my lip and looked down.

Susie looked at me curiously. "I knew it," she cried.

"Knew what?"

"Oh, don't play dumb with me. I can see it. You're glowing all over. You're carrying his child, aren't you? I've been there, you know. I know the symptoms."

"Please don't let on to Chris that you know. We've decided to keep it secret for a while."

"And that doesn't bother you?"

"Why? Should it?"

"I don't know. Is he working on his divorce?"

"He says he is."

Susie didn't say any more, but I couldn't help wondering once again why the divorce was taking so long.

We both watched Chris and Ashley coming back hand in hand. I looked at Susie. "You know he still misses his little girl."

"Yes, I can imagine. The loss of a child is something you will never forget."

"That's why I think he'll be a good father."

"I hope you're right."

I knew I was right. He might stop caring for me, but he'd never stop caring for his child. In fact, he'd probably like to have another little girl.

Carmen was as spectacular as the reviews had said, and Chris did his best to stay engaged. Ashley sat next to him on the other side, and I could tell she was taken with him.

"How did you like it?" I asked Chris afterwards.

"Good. At least I understood the story, but I didn't think Carmen was attractive enough to be able to hook these two guys. Don José should have stayed with his much prettier and more loyal fiancée. And then all this singing, and in French!"

"But the one who sang Carmen had a lovely voice," Susie said. "And that's what counts in opera."

"And see what happens when someone lets himself be consumed by passionate rage," I added.

"Why do I have the feeling that somehow this has something to do with me?" Chris asked.

"It has to do with all of us," I said. "Great works like *Carmen* always explore human vices and virtues. Susie can teach you more than I can. She already has her PhD."

"Which you'll have soon too, right?"

"Maybe."

We took Susie and Ashley home and drove to my place.

"I'll stay till Tuesday, if it's okay with you. When will you be home tomorrow?"

"Early, since I don't have much to prepare for Tuesday."

"I'll have dinner ready for you."

"Great! That's just what I need, a house husband."

In my first class on Monday morning, right in front, to my distraction, sat the most handsome student I've ever seen...an Italian-looking, younger version of Chris.

"How am I supposed to concentrate on my lecture?" I asked Alan and Kevin, who had offices next to mine, as we commiserated during lunch.

The afternoon class had a lot of Chinese students. "They're taking over our colleges too," I complained to Chris, who had grilled steaks and a good salad ready for me when I came home.

"That's too bad," he commented. "Isn't the school supposed to be a community college? With free tuition, paid for with our tax money."

"It's not free for the international students," I said. "They pay full price and then some. That's why they're recruited. The community colleges are underfunded, or so they say, and they make up some of the deficit with money from foreign students. And these students do contribute to our economy in general as well. Do you know what kind of cars they drive?"

"I've no idea."

"Porsches, Maseratis, Mercedes, and I even saw an Aston Martin in the parking lot today. Kevin, my younger friend—you remember Kevin, don't you?"

"Yeah, I remember him."

"Well, he told me that car is worth a couple of hundred thousand dollars."

"That's right. New. It's a two-hundred-thousand-dollar car new."

"The faculty lot is full of Toyotas, Hondas, a few Fords, and my lone Subaru, while the student lots are filled with expensive cars. Many of the domestic students don't even have cars, and those who do often park on the street to save the parking fee the school charges. Kevin says that the UCI parking lot is like this too. But enough about school. What did you do all day?"

"I took the Packard out for a drive. A few people came up to look at it in the parking lot when I went grocery shopping."

It struck me that we already sounded like an old, married couple.

Chris left the following morning but returned late Saturday night, then left again on Sunday night, a pattern he kept until our birthday. He wanted to make sure his jobs around the resort were completed before it turned cold. I had kept a journal most of the summer but didn't take the time to write much in it during that time. However, I remember he called in the evening of the 17th of September, and we wished each other happy birthday.

CHAPTER TWENTY-THREE

OUR BIRTHDAY PARTY

Our birthday fell on a Thursday, and I drove up to Chris's place on Friday afternoon—the eighteenth. The deciduous trees were already starting to turn yellow and red, adding a different beauty to the place. It was windy, and a lot of leaves had fallen to the ground.

I had been wondering what kind of birthday present to buy for Chris, and I also wondered whether he would get anything for me. If he hadn't, I decided I wouldn't embarrass him with a present from me, but I wanted to have something ready just in case. I finally hit on the idea of giving him the Rolex watch I had bought for Robert from my royal pawnbroker friend in Riyadh. It was used, but you couldn't really tell, and Robert had only worn it once or twice. I put it in a box and wrapped it up. Then I copied Elizabeth Browning's sonnet 43, *How do I love thee?* in tiny script on a small card.

Maria was still at the house when I arrived. "Miss Megan, happy birthday. I'm so happy about the baby," she said in her charming, accented English, and she laid her hand on my tummy. "I'm like mummy to Chris, you know. I'll be like grandma to baby."

"*Gracias*, Maria. I'm very happy too."

"I make tamales," she said as she got ready to leave.

"*Gracias*," I said again and poured myself a glass of juice. "*Hasta luego.*"

"*Adios.*"

When Chris came home, we wished each other happy birthday again, but he had no present, so I kept the watch in my purse.

"I've made reservations at Settlers Inn for tomorrow night," he said. "Ed, Elizabeth, and James are coming and maybe Joe and Sandy and Cheryl and Jonathan."

"Wow!"

"You don't mind, do you? Cheryl has been such a help to me, cleaning my scar when it got infected and bringing me different ointments, so I can't ignore her and her husband."

"No, that's nice. I like them all."

"Good."

We arrived before the others, and Al had a large table set with a bouquet of roses in the middle. "Be careful! They have nasty thorns," Chris warned as I tried to smell them.

All of the others except James came shortly afterwards. Cheryl looked at me funny, I thought. Like Susie, she probably picked up on any little clue and knew what was going on.

Everyone had wine except me, and Chris drank only one glass. They all had presents that we opened after we had finished the main course of steak and lobster tails—a clay sculpture of a bald eagle in flight from Sandy and Joe, an alarm clock with all kinds of gadgets from Ed and Elizabeth, and an earthquake emergency kit from Cheryl and Jonathan. We were probably difficult people to buy presents for, and I'm sure they were thankful they could buy *one* present for both of us.

Then Chris took out an envelope from his jacket pocket and gave it to me. I turned it around. A card maybe, with his own poem? A gift card perhaps? Surely not money. I opened it and pulled out a rumpled pink paper. The pink slip to the old Packard. I didn't know what to say except "Thank you." And I gave Chris a hug. Then I pulled myself together. "I guess I'm now the official owner of an antique car that's been hiding out in my garage."

Everyone laughed.

"It's certainly the most original gift I've ever received," I said.

"I'm sure you can work the car into your next mystery plot," Joe said.

"Maybe," I said. "I could call it The Mystery of President Roosevelt's car."

"Sandy and I just read your last book, and it's pretty good," Joe continued.

"Thank you."

"And now I understand you have another one finished. How do you come up with ideas?"

"Some are based on real cases, unsolved cases preferably."

"I have something else for you too," Chris said. He took out a little blue velvety box from his pants pocket and gave it to me. It was obviously a ring, and everyone was watching as I opened the box. Staring me in the face was a sparkling, blood-red ruby ring, not too big a stone as to look gaudy, but rather a size that I could actually wear, set with chips of rubies and diamonds. I slipped it on my left ring finger. "It's beautiful," I said and showed it around.

"The jeweler said it was a genuine stone from Burma, and he even gave me a certificate. That's all I know."

"It's the color called pigeon-blood, and stones of that color are mainly found in Burma, which is now called Myanmar."

"Oh, that's right. You know about gemstones; I'd forgotten that."

"Just a little bit, and it fits me perfectly. How did you know my ring size?"

"I picked up your wedding band from the soap dish, remember?"

"You saved my wedding ring?"

"Yeah, you didn't want me to throw it away, did you? You may need it again."

"Oh, you're impossible," I said and slapped his hand.

"There's a note in the box too," he said. "Read it."

I unfolded the paper, thinking it was the certificate from the jeweler, but instead it was the typed version of the story Chris had written in my writing workshop almost four months ago. I read it: *We met over broken sprinklers, but unlike the girl in the poem, she had no rouge on her cheeks or gloves on her hands because she is a sporty type with a good body, big blue eyes, and golden unruly hair, so I called her Goldilocks. After I fixed the sprinkler heads, we had our first date over coffee….*

"But you didn't finish it," I said.

"As I recall, *you* were supposed to finish it. You're the writer."

I folded the paper up again and put it back in the box.

"And I have something for you too," I said as I took out the little box

151

and the tiny card on which I had copied the lovely sonnet and gave it to him. He read the poem slowly and with great feeling:

How do I love thee? Let me count the ways.
I love thee to the depth and breadth and height
My soul can reach, when feeling out of sight
For the ends of being and ideal grace.
I love thee to the level of every day's
Most quiet need, by sun and candle-light.
I love thee freely, as men strive for right.
I love thee purely, as they turn from praise.
I love thee with the passion put to use
In my old griefs, and with my childhood's faith.
I love thee with a love I seemed to lose
With my lost saints. I love thee with the breath,
Smiles, tears, of all my life; and, if God choose,
I shall but love thee better after death.

"Wow," Elizabeth said. "That gives me goose bumps. Did you write that?"

"No, I borrowed it from the 19th century English poet Elizabeth Browning, who wrote it for her lover."

"I thought it sounded familiar," Sandy said.

Chris opened the box and took out the gold watch. "Rolex," he read out loud as he stared at the face of it. "A gold Rolex! Where on earth did you get that?"

"I have my ways."

"I'll be darned," Joe exclaimed.

"Actually, it used to belong to an Arabian prince who pawned it to a friend of mine. I got it, and I'm giving it to another prince charming."

I saw the disbelief on their faces.

"That's the problem with you writers," Joe said laughingly. "We never know what the truth is and what you make up on the spot."

"Oh, Chris didn't tell you that I lived in the Middle East, including Saudi Arabia, where my husband was the corporate pilot for one of the elder Bin Laden's many grandsons."

"As in Osama Bin Laden?" Cheryl asked incredulously.

"Yes, one of his nephews. The elder Bin Laden had over fifty sons and probably as many daughters, except they didn't count the girls at that time. Then these sons had children, so now there are a couple of thousand Bin Ladens around, and they're not all terrorists, of course, but rather ordinary, although very wealthy businessmen, and for a while, my husband was a pilot for one of them. Actually, this Bin Laden relative owned a construction company, I remember, or maybe several companies; and my husband made enough on that gig to buy our house and the cabin. Most of the time, he flew his own small plane hauling people and cargo all over Africa. He died in a plane crash over there."

"Yes, we heard about that," Elizabeth said. "It must have been a terrible shock for you, but we didn't hear the Bin Laden story,"

"And now, enough of a thousand-and-one Arabian nights! It's time for cake." Chris announced. I had taken center stage for as long as he could handle, and he motioned to our waitress, who brought in a baked Alaska with a myriad of candles as most of the patrons in the restaurant sang *Happy Birthday* in three or four different keys. No one apparently paid attention to the copyright law up here. We finished off with coffee.

"I think it's time for us to leave the birthday girl and boy alone," Ed said decisively, and everyone got ready to leave.

"You're staying over, aren't you?" Chris said to Joe and Sandy.

"Yeah, if that's all right with Megan," Joe answered and looked at me.

"Of course," I said. "That house is big enough for an army."

"How do you like it there?"

"Oh, it's beautiful, and Chris tells me that you built it yourself."

"Yeah, I was in better shape back then." He picked up his cane and walked fairly steadily across the floor.

It was chilly outside, and when we returned home, Chris lit a fire in the fireplace. "Maria thought you might get cold," Chris said. "So, she carried in the wood and made everything ready."

We sat and watched the flames for a while before Joe and Sandy went upstairs. I was so tired I could have gone to sleep on the big couch, but Chris pulled me up, and I woke up just long enough to get properly prepared for bed.

CHAPTER TWENTY-FOUR

THE ESCAPE

Right after Midterm, we had a few days off, and I invited Susie and her daughter to come up and spend the weekend with us at Chris's place. Although some trees had shed their leaves already, many were still flaming red and yellow, while the pine trees stayed green, of course. The lake was as cold and blue as a sapphire, and at this time we might be able to see bald eagles.

"This is not a cabin; it's a mansion," Susie exclaimed when she saw the house. Both mother and daughter looked sporty and very much alike in ponytails and multi-colored loose tops over dark stretch pants.

"Those were my exact words when I first saw the place too," I said, and I gave them both a tour. Chris was not home yet, and Maria was getting ready to leave, so we had the whole house to ourselves. We said hello to Duchess first, and I told Ashley she could take her for a walk in the morning. Ashley was fascinated by the gym, and so we all took turns on the different machines before we had snacks on the deck and Susie entertained us on the piano. After a while, Ashley ran down to the boat, and when Chris came home, he took Ashley fishing. They came home with another rainbow trout.

"I promised Ashley we could have this for supper," Chris announced. "We can have what Maria made tomorrow." And he and Ashley cleaned and cooked the fish.

"I thought you didn't like fish," Susie said teasingly to Ashley.

"I like this kind."

"It's amazing how much better fish tastes when you've caught it yourself," I said.

Maria had already put wood in the fireplace, and we soon had a roaring fire going. Ashley proudly presented Chris with a wallet made out of brown, speckled duct tape, which he accepted with amazement. Then we spent the evening playing Clue, one of my favorite games.

"Do you want to sleep in the same room or separate rooms?" Chris asked Susie as he walked with them upstairs.

"One room will be fine," Susie answered.

I wondered if she was afraid Chris would pay Ashley a visit during the night if she had her own room.

After breakfast and after Ashley had taken Duchess for a walk, we all went out on the boat, and Chris and Ashley were at the helm while I tried to be the guide, telling Susie about all the famous people who lived in the big lake-front homes. I was on the lookout for bald eagles.

They left early as Ashley had school the next day. Chris took time off until I left on Tuesday afternoon. He would come down on Saturday as usual.

It was a couple of weeks later when I was searching the Internet for an article written by a colleague that I saw the headline, *Two more patients escape from Patton State Hospital in San Bernardino*. It was the asylum that housed Chris's wife, so I read on with some trepidation:

SAN BERNARDINO, CA: Causing outrage among local residents, two more dangerous criminals, a man and a woman, were reported missing Monday from Patton State Mental Hospital in San Bernardino, the facility that treats the criminally insane. The new escapees raise to seven the number of patients who have slipped away from the facility in the past month. None of them have been recaptured.

Both escapees were discovered missing during a bed check early Monday morning, but it is believed they exited the facility Sunday night. How the convicts escaped is still under investigation, but according to a hospital spokesperson, the woman apparently picked several locks to get out of her unit, while the male convict may have been on the grounds and not in his unit. To get through a fourteen-foot fence fortified with barbed wire and cut glass, they reportedly used wire cutters and other tools left at the facility by a construction crew who had recently worked at the aging hospital at the base of the San Bernardino Mountains about sixty miles east of Los Angeles.

"They have the potential to be dangerous," the spokesperson said. "We don't know if they were armed when they left the hospital."

The man was identified as Thomas Wilson, thirty-one, convicted of raping several women at knife point. The woman was identified as Amanda Cronin, thirty-five, convicted of attempted murder of her husband, a well-known contractor in the mountain town of Running Springs.

The spokesperson said that so far this year over thirty patients have escaped from the facility. Most of them get away while they are on hospital grounds rather than locked up in their units. Those who escape during so-called "therapeutic community outings" have caused the most concern. One escapee convicted of armed burglary disappeared inside a Target store. The hospital, which is filled to its capacity of 1187 licensed beds, is now on lockdown.

"There is no cure for the criminally insane, most of whom suffer from psychotic schizophrenia," said a hospital doctor who asked to remain anonymous because he was not authorized to speak publicly. "One patient convicted of killing a child was released recently to stay with her brother, because she promised to take her medication and stay out of trouble, but after a week she assaulted her five-year-old niece and was brought back here by her family."

I immediately called Chris: "Did you hear the news?" I asked.

"Yes, they called from the hospital yesterday, and I went down there right away."

"Why?"

"I wanted to get more details from some of the people I know in her unit. I thought they might have some idea where she and that other guy had gone."

"Why didn't you call me?"

"I thought she would have been recaptured by now."

"She's probably already up at the resort. Where are you?"

"I'm in Redlands and will stay with Joe tonight."

"She'll be looking for you at your house, so don't go there," I said. In my mind, I had an image of this crazy woman running around his kitchen with a carving knife. "Stay at my cabin if you go up there."

"That's probably a good idea. Ed has put a deputy at both my father-in-law's office and his house. He'll keep an eye on my house himself, he said."

"Good."

"We've also posted a 25,000-dollar reward for information leading to her arrest. Maybe that will help."

"Wow! Do you think there's a possibility that she knows about me? Could this Maddie have told her, for example?"

"I don't think they've stayed in touch, and neither one will know where you live. She'll contact her father for sure. If they don't find her tonight, I'll go up and see what I can get out of Annette. And don't call me. I'll call you when I have more news."

"Okay, I won't. I'll text you if I hear anything on the news. Is there anything I can do?"

"No, just stay away. She's dangerous."

"I know that, but I don't think she'll go after me. She's obsessed with you, and if they're still together, her boyfriend may have a gun."

"I know."

I told him I loved him and hung up. Although I had my students to think about, I scoured the Internet for information between classes; and when I Googled it, I found a small notice about the reward, but nothing else. This was LA, and crime was not exactly hot news, and a prison escape kept people's interest for no more than a day or two.

Chris called again the next afternoon after my last class. "Now my father-in-law is also missing," he said. "I almost strangled Annette to get her to talk, but all she knows is that he'd told her he'd be gone for a couple of days and not to call him. I made her call him anyway, but there was no answer, and I think he may have locked up his phone in a drawer so he can't be traced."

"Did he go off the mountain then?"

"Where else could he go? Ed has put out an APB on him. He evidently took his own car."

A little later I received another update: It turned out that Chris's father-in-law had been spotted driving east toward Big Bear and not down the hill on highway eighteen as first assumed.

"He may go down the mountain on the other side to throw the sheriff off," I suggested.

"They're following up on every lead," Chris said. "But so far there's no trace of him *on* or *off* the mountain. Annette told one of the deputies that he had withdrawn five thousand dollars in cash before he left."

"Probably so no one could trace his credit card transactions."

"Maybe."

"And where are you right now?"

"With Ed, and don't worry. I'm not going to my place. I'll sleep over in your cabin."

"Good. I wish I could be there with you."

The next day, there were more developments. The father-in-law's car had been discovered abandoned in a restaurant parking lot in Big Bear, but he was not believed to have visited that establishment.

Meanwhile, a car rental agency reported that he had rented a Chrysler SUV from them for a week.

"He must be crazy to think he can elude law enforcement for any length of time in this day and age," I said to Chris when he called. "They'll soon find the rental car, and when they do, he may be charged with aiding and abetting a criminal. What kind of lawyer is this guy?"

The police did spot the rental car on the way to Las Vegas the next day and gave a short chase. However, the father-in-law had quickly pulled over and had evidently explained that he was going to Las Vegas on business and that his own car had stalled in Big Bear. The cash was for an associate, and so they let him go.

"I did give a girl in Amanda's unit some money to give to Amanda a few weeks ago," Chris said.

"Why?"

"She had asked for it, and I thought she needed it for some creams and stuff she used to use."

"How much?" I asked.

"Just a couple of hundred dollars."

"Oh, my God! Maybe the two of them have gone to Las Vegas to try to make more money before they come after you."

"Actually, two people fitting their descriptions have also been spotted in downtown Los Angeles, near Fifth and Los Angeles Streets" Chris said.

"How would they've gotten there, or to Las Vegas for that matter?" I wondered out loud, trying to think of ways.

"The boyfriend may have hot-wired a car. Several cars have been reported stolen in the San Bernardino area the last few days. One was found in Los Angeles. I'll go down there tomorrow to look around for places that a woman like Amanda would most likely hang out in."

"No, don't do that," I protested. "It's a big city, and it's too dangerous. Have you told Ed where you're planning to go?"

"No, he wouldn't approve."

"And for good reason," I said, but I knew he had already made up his mind. "Will you come over here afterwards then?"

"Okay."

We said good-bye and hung up.

It was early Saturday evening when he finally arrived. To my surprise, he didn't immediately remove his jacket as he usually did as soon as he came inside. When I touched his right side, I felt something hard.

"What's this?" I asked suspiciously.

"My gun."

"Your gun?" I exclaimed in disbelief and also with some fear.

"Yeah, I told you, I have a permit. It's perfectly legal."

"You went around downtown LA with a loaded gun? What would you have done if you'd spotted her? Shot her?"

"If she'd tried to attack me," he said. "If I'd had a gun when she first tried to kill me, all this could have been avoided."

"And you would have been accused of murder."

"It would have been self-defense. But it's no use talking about that now." He sighed with an air of resignation and gave me his jacket to hang up before he placed his gun on the coffee table and sat down on the couch. I sat down next to him and took his hand.

"I met a couple of nice officers down there," he continued. "I told them who I was, and I told them about my brother."

"Did they stop you?"

"No, I stopped them. They confirmed the APB on Amanda and the tip that she'd been spotted on 5th Street, evidently a notorious spot for drug dealing. They promised to keep their eyes open. And they advised me to leave everything to them, and so I left and came here."

"That was a smart decision," I agreed. His face looked haggard and thinner. He'd lost some weight, and his eyes had lost some of their glitter.

"I'm sorry I've dragged you into all of this, Megan," he said as he pulled me toward him and kissed the top of my head.

"You haven't dragged me into anything," I said. "As you may recall, I *chose* to come back to you because I love you. And there's that other little thing: I'm carrying your child."

"You're a brave woman. I don't know what you see in me."

"Oh, stop it. Please don't talk like that. You're a wonderful man, and I'm crazy about you."

That confession brought a faint smile to his face.

"This is just a temporary setback," I continued. "And we'll get through this together." I paused and smiled. "I told you I saw the doctor yesterday, and everything is fine with the baby. He's already starting to kick and move around, and when the nurse performed the ultrasound, she also took pictures of the baby." I went over to my purse and found the envelope with the photos that I then showed to Chris. He wasn't particularly impressed.

"It looks like a helpless little frog," he said.

"The nurse thought it was a boy," I said, "although she warned that it could just be a finger down there."

That information brightened his face considerably.

"And now I think you're hungry," I said. "With my limited cooking ability, I fried some chicken and made a potato salad earlier today. I've set the table in the kitchen. Let's go and have a bite to eat. Then we can go for an evening stroll before we go to bed."

I went into the kitchen ahead of him, lit a candle, brought out a bottle of Cabernet, and poured him a glass.

He ate and drank heartily and was soon back to his lighthearted self. For a couple of days, we were able to relax and forget about this whole sordid affair–enjoy quiet meals, make love, and go for long walks.

Sunday evening, Chris called Ed and learned that a motel in Riverside had reported that a man and a woman fitting the descriptions given by the hospital had rented a room for three days and paid cash in advance, but by the time the detectives showed up, they had disappeared.

"They're bound to trip up sooner or later," I said. "Why don't you go about your work as usual? I know that's easier said than done, but we can trade cars, and you can stay with your dad or at my cabin or here. Let's just wait this out." But I remembered the line from the newspaper: "None of the escapees have been recaptured," referring to all who had escaped this year. However, this constant chase and worrying weren't leading anywhere either.

Meanwhile, the father-in-law was back at the resort, Ed reported. Deputies had questioned him, but it was unclear what he had done in Las Vegas and who the associate was that had received such a large sum of money in cash. This father-in-law was obviously a slick customer. If he had somehow given his daughter money, he ran a huge risk of being charged with conspiracy and obstruction of justice, and he surely knew that.

Chris agreed. He returned to work early Monday morning, and I immersed myself in school work.

One day I read on the Internet that Thomas Wilson, Amanda's companion, convicted of rape at knife point, had returned to Patton of his own volition, brought there by a relative. Chris went down to try to talk to him. A detective had also interrogated him, but Wilson said he had left Amanda after the first day, and his family corroborated his story.

Amanda would have had no place to go but back to her father's place or to Chris's house, and a day later Chris called and said that she had evidently been spotted in the resort town but had managed to disappear once again. She was reportedly not at her father's place.

"Does she still have old friends around?" I asked.

"Maybe. There are a lot of hermits and lone woodsmen around that might take her in."

By now I had applied for and received a leave of absence for the spring semester, not only to have the baby, but also to write another novel. In the middle of November, I gave my students assignments for independent study and decided to drive up and surprise Chris. Several weeks had passed since the escape, and Amanda must have been taken in by somebody, or she might be dead.

Chris was not entirely pleased to see me at first, but I promised to be careful, and all was quiet. I spent some time with Cindy, and Chris and I settled with her on the painting of the island in the lake that Chris and I had raced to during my first outing with his boat on the lake.

I also wanted to talk to Ed face-to-face to get his true take on the story. Did he think this woman was as dangerous as Chris believed? Was the father so arrogant that he believed he could hide the truth and his daughter without being found out? Annette seemed to have cooperated because she was afraid of getting caught up in her boss's shenanigans.

However, Ed had become distracted from the issue because Elizabeth had been diagnosed with breast cancer and was in the hospital for testing. There was no end to the drama this family had to endure.

I called Ed anyway. He was on his way home from the hospital, and he said he would stop by. He was still in his uniform and cut an imposing figure as he walked in through the door. I offered him coffee, but he declined.

"I'm so sorry about Elizabeth," I said. "How is she?"

"Not great."

"I'm sure she'll be okay. There's been a lot of good cancer research recently," I said to comfort him.

"That's true." He looked at me for a moment. "And how are you doing? You're carrying Chris's baby, I hear. What am I gonna do with this naughty little brother of mine?" He was surprisingly mild-mannered when we were just the two of us, and he didn't have to project such a macho image.

"I'm happy," I assured him. "You know, I was married for eight years and thought I couldn't have kids."

He smiled the same crooked smile that reminded me of Chris. He had the same facial features as Chris, although they were not put together in quite the same way. He was also a little taller and bigger overall, more rugged looking.

"Do you think Chris's father-in-law is involved in all of this, as I've heard?" I asked.

"Yes, we believe he is, and we'll prosecute him to the fullest if we can find evidence of that."

"What about Annette?"

"Oh, you know her too. Well, she's scared and is cooperating."

"Is Chris in danger, do you think?"

"Absolutely. Don't let him stay at the house. He can stay with me or here at your cabin or with our dad. She's obsessed with killing him. She hears voices telling her to do it, as she said at the trial."

"Do you think she's in town?"

"It's possible, but I don't see how she could survive this long on the run without help from someone. Her father may be helping her with money at least." He looked at the door. "Chris is coming home soon, right? I'd better go on home and see what James is up to. He's worried about his mother, of course. He's at a difficult age, and he understands that she may not survive. Both Chris and I know what it's like to lose our mom."

"I know," I said. "Is there anything I can do?"

"No, not at the moment, but thank you. Just take care of yourself, and stand by Chris."

"I will," I said. "Thank you for coming over." I gave him a hug, and he left.

CHAPTER TWENTY-FIVE

TRAGEDY STRIKES

C hris came down to my place in Los Angeles on Saturday afternoon and left Monday morning. His work schedule had slowed down some, and he had given up the wild goose chase of going after the crazy wife. Beaten down by the fateful flight and the fruitless manhunt, he had become a changed man, more subdued and circumspect, but little by little some of his cheerful demeanor returned. Because my home in Los Angeles was far away from the epicenter of the search, he felt safe there with me. Up at the resort, he was constantly looking over his shoulder in case she should show up.

Since school was closed the entire Thanksgiving weekend, I decided to drive up Monday after Chris had left. I texted him when I arrived at my cabin, and he called right back. "You shouldn't have come up here," he said, and he did not sound pleased. "It's still not over."

"But at one point we have to try to live somewhat normal lives," I countered. "She surely is either lost somewhere or dead by now."

"No one has found a body fitting her description, and until they do, we should be prepared for the worst."

"I know, but you'll be safe here at my place."

He came over after work, and we had roasted chicken already cooked at the store, and he admitted he was happy to see me. Not even Duchess knew where he was as Maria's family had volunteered to take care of her.

My journal, which I had misplaced somewhere, was not at my cabin as I'd hoped, and the next day I decided to walk over to Chris's house to look for it there. It was chilly, and I buttoned my coat and was glad I had brought a woolen scarf and gloves. No one was around, and all was quiet. Although the main entrance was locked, I was surprised to find one of the side doors open. I thought Chris had told one of his men to change all the locks in case she had one of the original keys hidden somewhere. I walked in through the kitchen and into the living room. The house was cold, so I went over to the thermostat and turned it up to sixty-eight degrees. Then I peeked into the dog pen; but, of course, Duchess was with Maria's family, and I made a mental note to myself to offer to take care of her after school was out in December.

Back in the kitchen, I noticed a dirty plate and a cup in the sink. I wondered if Chris had been there, but he would never have left dirty dishes out. I opened the fridge. Not a crumb left. I didn't think Maria had been here either, but someone must have cleaned out the fridge and pantry. The perennial problem up here was, of course, squatters moving into empty houses, eating everything in sight and leaving a mess, taking any valuables, if there were any, with them when they left—although seldom wantonly destroying the property.

Suddenly I heard a creaking noise from somewhere and stopped to listen, but I thought I must have left the side door open, letting a strong gust of wind blow through the house. I was not brave enough to venture upstairs to check out the bedrooms and TV room because the house had never made me feel completely comfortable. I found my journal on Chris's desk in his office and got ready to leave, but the grand piano beckoned and, although I knew I shouldn't be here, I removed my gloves, loosened my scarf, and sat down to play a few chords, then a few pieces I remembered. However, after a few minutes I smelled gasoline coming from somewhere. I stopped playing and sniffed a few times. The smell seemed to be coming from the upstairs.

Suddenly, I heard a door open and immediately slam shut. I froze for a moment, and then slowly turned around. At the top of the stairs, stood a ragged-looking woman in a heavy dark coat with matted brown hair shooting up from the top of her head like a volcano. A pair of wild eyes was staring at me. Although she looked nothing like the picture Chris had shown around, I knew immediately who she was. This woman was a real lunatic.

"Who are you?" she shouted down at me in a hoarse voice.

"Just a friend," I said calmly and tried to smile and look friendly. "I'll be out of here right away." I carefully gathered up my purse, my gloves, and scarf that had slipped off and fallen onto the piano bench before backing out toward the kitchen and the side door in case the front door had been bolted shut.

She came slowly down the stairs. "I know who you are, bitch," she said as I was walking backward, facing her as if I were trying to escape from an encounter with a threatening black bear. Once outside, I slammed the side door shut and started running toward the road, fumbling for my phone in my purse. Hands shaking, I dialed 9-1-1. "This is Megan Viets," I said breathlessly. "I've discovered the location of the fugitive Amanda Cronin." I gave the address.

"The sheriff is on his way," the operator responded after a short pause. "Are you okay?"

"Yes."

"Where are you exactly?"

I told her.

"What happened?"

I told her the story.

"Stay on the line with me, and stay calm. Help is on the way."

"Okay." I turned around and looked up at the house. Smoke was billowing out of an open upstairs window. "Oh, my God. She's set fire to the place," I shouted into the phone. "Please send the fire department too."

There was another short pause. "They're on their way, Ma'am. Stay where you are and don't get involved. Help is on the way. They'll be there momentarily."

"I need to call my fiancée, the owner of the house," I said and hung up.

Chris picked up the phone immediately. "She's here!" I shouted desperately into the phone.

"Whoa! Hold on! Who? Where?"

"Your wife. She's set your house on fire. I've called 9-1-1. The fire department and the sheriff are on their way."

"Where the hell are you?"

"I'm up on the road from your house. She's inside, and she looks terrible. She hasn't seen soap and water for weeks."

"Damn! But what are you doing over there? Get the hell away. I'll be right over."

"No, you stay away too. Help is on the way. There's nothing you can do." But, of course, I knew he wouldn't listen. Why had I even called him?

I heard sirens blaring from all directions. Two sheriff's cars followed but Ed arrived first. Then two fire engines came roaring down the road, and before they'd come to a complete stop, firefighters in heavy gear spilled out with hoses that they connected to fire hydrants before running into the burning house. Flames now spewed out of the upstairs windows, licking the high outside walls.

Chris came, but he didn't see me. I heard Ed shouting to him in his booming voice to stay away. "Look after Megan. We'll handle this." But there was no use talking to Chris, who ran inside unprotected among the firefighters and deputies. I didn't notice whether he had his gun drawn or not, but in the mass confusion, I heard at least half a dozen gun shots. "Oh, my God!" I thought. "He's finally shot her. Or even scarier, she had killed Chris. Why does he always think he has to take charge?"

I felt dizzy and must have blacked out because the next thing I knew I was on a stretcher with a paramedic on each side of me taking my blood pressure and checking my pulse. "What happened?" I asked.

"You passed out," one of the paramedics answered.

"What happened to Chris? Do you know Chris Cronin?"

"Yes, we know Chris. He's alive but badly hurt. He's being carried to the ambulance over there." He pointed to an ambulance that I could see only in a blur.

"What happened to the woman?"

"From what we know so far, she lunged at Chris with a knife, and one of the deputies shot her dead."

"Oh, wow! So she's finally dead. Did she cut him open again?"

"No, evidently she never reached him, but a burning beam fell on him," the paramedic informed me. "We don't know how badly he's injured. He may be airlifted to a bigger hospital in Colton." He finished checking my vital signs and covered me up. "As soon as they leave, we'll take you to the local hospital to check you out, but don't worry. You'll be fine."

At the hospital, I was placed in a room right away, and a young female doctor came in and talked to me. I was fine, she said, and after she left, Cheryl, who was on duty, came in. "I'll take you home if you want me to," she offered.

"Thank you, Cheryl. Do you know anything about what happened to Chris?"

"No, he was airlifted to Colton. Ed and Joe are on their way. "

Joe, or even Ed, was, of course, the next of kin. I was not in the picture. That was one advantage of being formally married. The spouse was the one called.

It was late in the evening before Ed called. "It doesn't look good," he said. "His spine is injured, but we don't know if it's just a bruise or a contusion, as the doctor called it, or if it's more serious. We'll know more tomorrow."

"Thank you, Ed. I heard you yelling at him not to go in. I'm sorry he didn't listen."

"Yes, I know. He's always been stubborn. We'll update you tomorrow. Joe will stay here tonight."

I went to bed but couldn't fall asleep for a long time, although I kept telling myself there was nothing I could do. I should have stayed away, and Chris shouldn't have gone in, but it was done and over with. No use thinking about that now. There was nothing I could do to change it, nothing I could do but wait.

Ed called again the next day. "In addition to the bruise, there's a small crack in the spine," he reported. "There's nothing the doctors can do at the moment; sometimes the crack heals by itself, the doctor in charge told us. It will be two or three weeks before they can tell."

"Can I come over?"

"Why don't you wait until tomorrow? Joe will go home and get some sleep. I'll go home and see how James is. Elizabeth is not doing that great, but we'll all come over tomorrow and celebrate Thanksgiving in the hospital."

I was tempted to ignore Ed and go to the hospital anyway, but remembered that heeding Ed's advice had up to now been the best policy. The hospital staff might not even let me see Chris since I was not a relative.

CHAPTER TWENTY-SIX

AT THE HOSPITAL

The next morning, I left early and made good time because there was hardly any traffic. The underground parking structure was only half-full, and a short walk brought me to the reception desk, where I was given a badge and shown the way to Chris's intensive-care unit. The nurse on duty, a stout, capable-looking woman about forty years of age, said she was happy to have an extra body there since the hospital was short-staffed during the holiday weekend. I introduced myself as Chris's fiancée, and she led me up to the second floor. She left me at the door to his room.

He was lying in the bed with his eyes closed. My heart ached as I just stood there watching him. He hadn't shaved, so dark stubble framed his face, and his hair was matted, but to me he looked as handsome as ever. "Hi, honey," I said and touched his forehead, but he didn't respond.

I carried a chair over to the bedside and just sat there looking at him. The same nurse peeked in and waved, and I noticed from her badge that her name was Becky, R.N. I quickly followed her down the hall to find out if he was sleeping or just resting.

"He's sedated so he won't move unnecessarily, but he should wake up soon."

When I returned, he stirred and slowly opened his eyes; and when he saw me he smiled faintly and slowly held out his arms to me as I bent down to kiss him. "Does it hurt anywhere?" I asked.

"No, I'm sure they've shot me full of morphine so I can't feel anything," he said in a weak voice. He was obviously a little groggy still.

"Can you eat anything?"

"No, I'm not hungry, just tired."

I remained silent for a few moments. "At least the crazy woman is dead," I said finally. "You don't have to constantly be on guard anymore. You'll have nightmares about it for a while, I'm sure, but we'll get through this too."

His eyes were closing again, and I continued talking softly. "I don't know how long you'll have to stay in the hospital, but when the doctors release you, I can take care of you at home," I said. "School will be out soon." Of course, I wondered how much damage there was to the house and how soon the damage could be repaired. Joe would know.

Joe and Sandy came for a little while in the afternoon, and Ed came by himself, but Chris was too tired to talk. Since there was no update from the doctors because of the holiday, they left early. I left in the evening, but I returned the next morning and the next day as well. I skipped Thanksgiving dinner at Ed's house; I didn't feel like driving all the way up the mountain. Joe and Sandy as well as Cheryl had brought a turkey and trimmings to Ed and Elizabeth's place to keep everything as normal as possible for James's sake, but I decided to stay at the hospital. However, I needed to finish up at school and went home on Monday. Because I was not in top form and hardly performed at optimal capacity, I gave my students some slack too. I took their late papers, let them make up exams until the very end, and graded their assignments less harshly.

Joe kept me updated and also oversaw the restoration of the house that had already begun. We agreed that I would come out and sit with Chris on Sunday, and to my relief, by Sunday, Chris's condition already seemed much improved. "You look a lot better," I said encouragingly as I embraced him. He had shaved and there was more color in his cheeks.

"They'll keep me here at least four weeks, and then rehab," he said quietly, but his voice was less groggy.

"Maybe we can get physical therapy at home instead," I suggested. "One doctor friend told me that these rehabs are the pits, staffed with the worst doctors and caregivers. He said that if there's a half-witted wife at the house, the patient is better off at home with her." I paused and smiled at him. "Do you still want me to be your half-witted wife?"

He remained silent.

"I can understand how you've been badly burnt and may never want to commit yourself again; but, like me, I believe you're a bit old-fashioned too and don't want your son to be shuttled back and forth between his mother and father."

"But I don't have anything to offer you."

"Why do you have to offer me anything?"

"I don't know."

"Can't you just let me take charge for a while? I know you like to take care of people, but now it's time for me to take care of *you*."

He just stared at me blankly, and I started to fear that he was going to reject me. I showed him my ruby ring.

"Do you remember our birthday party?" I waited until he answered.

"Yeah, I remember."

I patted my tummy. "We can't so easily pick up and leave each other now," I said. "I won't let you go, you know. Do you think I want to deprive my son of his dad? I'm not going through this alone. You have a part in it too. Remember what you said after my writing workshop? You told me to write how I wanted our relationship to continue."

"I remember," he said and smiled. I remained silent, waiting for some further comment.

"How should it go then?" he finally said.

"They married—or at least they lived together—and dedicated their lives to their handsome son, who grew up to become the president of the United States."

He looked at me with a tired and pensive expression, and I took his hand.

"But don't think about all this now," I said. "Just concentrate on getting better." I paused and then changed the subject: "Joe said the work to repair the fire damage on your house is already in progress." I tried to sound more cheerful. "The insurance adjuster has been there, and the men are raring to go to work, but Joe has probably told you that already. Next week school is out, and I plan to stay up there, either at my cabin or your house. I'll replace some of the damaged furniture, and prepare everything for when you come home."

It was hard to be upbeat, of course; the doctor had told Joe that if Chris didn't get back on his feet during the next couple of weeks, he might end up in a wheelchair for the rest of his life. I shuddered at the thought, but tried to brush it out of my universe.

The next time I saw Ed, I asked him if he had been able to figure out how Amanda had escaped the deputies for so long.

"She'd evidently broken into empty cabins and helped herself to whatever food was left," he said. "She also apparently got some money from the suspected small-time drug dealers around by giving them food and doing small favors for them. How she got into Chris's house beats me, but we found a tool that she must have used to pick locks." He looked serious. "I take some of the blame, and if this had been someone other than my brother, there would have been complaints."

"You've had Elizabeth to worry about too, Ed. Don't be too hard on yourself. At least the old witch is dead."

When I returned to the hospital, I asked Chris if he'd heard how Amanda had survived for so long.

"Yeah, it turned out the bitch had become an expert at picking locks. She broke into empty, isolated cabins, emptied refrigerators and cupboards and slept there too. She never needed to go shopping, but I still feel she had help; maybe from her father or from one or two of the hermit woodsmen who still live up in the national forest."

"I'm surprised none of the deputies checked those cabins."

"There are a lot of them, and only so many deputies, and Ed had to spend time with James and Elizabeth." Chris was not about to put any blame on his brother.

My new mystery novel came out just as we were turning in final grades. According to our agreement, the publisher sent me ten free copies to pass out to friends and relatives. I gave one to Susie before we left, and the rest I took with me up to the resort.

"My book came out," I announced proudly to Chris when I saw him. I held up a copy for him to see before I gave it to him. "Look at the dedication page: 'For Chris.'"

He dutifully looked at the page.

"Look at what I've written for you on the title page: 'For my favorite man. I love you.'"

"It's nice. Thank you." He looked at me curiously.

"How do you feel today?" I asked.

"About the same. I'm getting physical therapy, but I still have no feeling below the waist."

I sighed. It was going to be a long road. He lay still for a while. "Does it hurt?" I asked.

"No, but the doctor told me that I may not walk again."

"Nonsense. What do these doctors know anyway? And they certainly don't know you."

"That's true, but the spine is more seriously damaged and is not healing as they thought it might at first."

"There's so much new medical research and technology now," I said. "What they can do today is really amazing."

"True, but in any case it does put a damper on our plans for the future."

"How?"

"Well, you surely don't want to marry a cripple."

"Yes, I do, and it's not a decision I make just for myself, but for our son." I had waited so long for a baby, and I had really given up. Now I wanted to make the most of it. I wanted to secure his future, provide him with a mom and a dad, and not a mom who left his father because he was in a wheelchair.

"Ed says I shouldn't pressure you."

"You're certainly not pressuring me. It sounds more like you're rejecting me."

"You may be taking on more responsibility than you realize. We may never have sex again."

"We've had enough sex to last us a lifetime. Surely, you didn't fall in love with me just for sex." I paused. Heat rushed to my cheeks. "Listen to me," I continued. "You're depressed about this whole situation, unhappy about yourself, and now you're transferring that unhappiness to me. You may not feel the same about me, but I feel the same about you. I love you, and I'm not letting you off the hook." I had started to tremble, tears welled up in my eyes, and my voice was unsteady.

"I'll still be involved with the child."

"Chris, your talk is putting undue stress on me. We'll have to talk about this later when you feel a whole lot better." I was ready to start crying and got up to leave. "I have to go to the bathroom," I said.

When I was alone, I held onto the sink and had a good cry for a while. He'd probably never intended to commit to me, I thought. All these excuses about not getting a divorce, and now still stalling. But I would manage somehow. I could sell the stupid old car, live on the proceeds from that for a while, and then go to work like other single moms. Susie managed quite well. She'd be a good mentor. How could I have been so gullible?

When I returned to the room, Chris looked at me for a moment and held out his arms. "Come here," he said in a commanding voice. Then he embraced me the best he could. "Honey, you've been crying," he said more softly.

"I'm all right," I replied.

"I'm just testing you. I don't want you to stick with me because you feel sorry for me. I want to make sure you're not staying with me because you feel a sense of guilt or loyalty to me now that I'm no longer a catch."

"I've never thought you were a catch. If I'd been looking for a catch, I'd waited for a doctor or a professor as my mother suggested."

"She said that?"

"All mothers say that."

"I didn't know that."

"There are actually some things you don't know, Chris." I said teasingly.

"So, do you want to marry me then?" he said. "I can't get down on my knee as you can see." He looked up at me with his still glittering eyes.

"Yes, I've been waiting for that question a long time," I said and embraced him.

We started to make plans for a small wedding ceremony after Chris returned home in January.

Although the repairs on the downstairs were almost completed, and I had decorated the living room with Christmas ornaments and put up a small Christmas tree and some outside lights, we all—Joe, Sandy, Elizabeth, James, Ed, and I—celebrated most of Christmas Day in the hospital. I had brought a small holiday flower arrangement for Chris's nightstand, but presents would have to wait until he returned home. Chris was bantering with James, who stayed by his mother's side and made sure she was comfortable. I called my mother but didn't tell her anything about the baby or Chris's accident. She had received my book but hadn't read it yet.

In the early evening, we left so Chris could rest, and I suggested that we should all return to Chris's house. They agreed, and we had ready-made eggnog by the fire. I gave out copies of my book to everyone but realized that Joe would be the only one reading it. In return, they gave me practical things for the baby–little blue jumpsuits, a hat, a rattle, and blankets.

"We're going to get married as soon as he comes home from the hospital," I announced matter-of-factly, and I heard gasps as everyone's wide-eyed face turned toward me. I stood up to gather the wrapping paper, and Joe came over and gave me a big hug.

"You're a brave woman," he said simply. He was, of course, a concerned father, worried about his son's future.

"Congratulations!" everyone chimed in together as if on cue.

"Thank you."

Miraculously, the grand piano had been spared in the fire. It had been in storage during the repair work but it was now back in its regular place. After everyone left—Joe and Sandy were staying over at Ed's—I took out Chris's mother's old Christmas music and played the old familiar tunes. I made a mental note of calling the piano turner before going to bed in Chris's big king-size bed. How strange it would be to have him here next to me again.

The day after Christmas, I brought Duchess home. She was ecstatic to see me and rediscover her old dog pen. We went for walks together every afternoon after I returned from the hospital.

CHAPTER TWENTY-SEVEN

HOMECOMING

And so, the day of Chris's homecoming was finally here. Steadying myself on a ski pole, I walked carefully down the familiar path from my cabin to the lake. It was sunny, and the road was mostly dry except for a few patches of treacherous black ice in the many shady spots. The air was chilly, and I stopped to button the top buttons on my woolen coat. The lake lay there, midnight blue and still like a sheet of ice. The boats had been pulled out and put in storage a month ago, and I was thinking about all the fun we'd had last summer, picnicking on the boat, water skiing, and swimming. How carefree life had been back then! Even after Chris had told me that he was married to a crazy woman, I'd managed to shove it to the back of my mind. One must live in the moment.

The big house sat there quietly facing the lake. It had now been fully restored to its original grandeur, the inside with a fresh coat of white and beige paint. I took out my key and opened the stately front door. I hadn't been here for a few days, and the house was cold, so I turned the thermostat up before I took down the Christmas decorations and put out the tree. The new couch looked good in front of the fireplace, which still had a few black spots on it from the fire. The grand piano also had a couple of black marks on the side, I noticed now, but the piano tuner said it had not suffered any damage.

"The strings and hammers are all intact," he said. "It's a *grand* piano."
He laughed heartily at his own joke.

I took off my coat, put it on the couch and sat down to play a few
scales and chords, but the room was still too cold. The garage was the
warmest room in the house, and Chris's two remaining antique cars
looked in good shape. Maria had been here to clean, and in the kitchen all
the appliances were gleaming. Duchess started barking when she heard
me, and I went out in her pen to make sure she had water. I would feed
her later.

The master bedroom and bathroom had been spared, while the upstairs
had suffered the most damage. I went up the rebuilt staircase to inspect
the rooms once more. Joe and the workmen had done a great job of
restoring everything. I had bought new bedding for all the bedrooms and a
new big-screen television set and a big new couch for the TV room.
Everything was ready for the big homecoming. I actually felt more at
home here after the restoration. There was more of me here now.

I went downstairs again and into Chris's office. His desk was clean
because all his papers had been put into a box on the floor. I hadn't had
time to look at it all because I'd spent most of my spare time in the
hospital, but now I started going through it and noticed that many of the
invoices, bids, architectural drawings, and brochures had some water
damage, but surely at least the invoices and bids must have been saved on
computer discs anyway.

At the bottom of the box lay my old journal, which I must have left the
day I rushed out of the house before the disaster. I sat down on the office chair
and started leafing through the pages. So much had happened in the seven
months or so since that early June day when I first met Chris. Did I have any
regrets? Would I have done things differently if I could have had a glimpse
into the future? Maybe. But no one has been able to tame the wilderness that
is the future. We just wade in among the thorns and hope to find some roses.

I was still daydreaming when Maria arrived with her famous Mexican
casserole, one of Chris's favorites. Ed came immediately afterwards.

"How's the big mama today?" he said and gave my tummy a little
squeeze. "Are you sure there aren't two in there?" He was quite familiar
with me now. In this family, I realized, they stuck together, worked
together, and shared everything, although hopefully not each other's

wives. However, I did not need to fear that I'd have to do all the care-giving by myself.

I looked at my stomach. I must have looked grotesque because I felt enormous. "I'm kind of big, aren't I?" I said laughingly. Then more seriously: "How's Elizabeth?"

He shook his head. "Not good, but hanging in there."

Finally, a big van pulled up in front. Joe had been at the hospital to help Chris get ready, and one of Chris's men had been commissioned to drive the borrowed van. I was standing by the new couch as Chris wheeled himself through the entrance, beads of perspiration covering his forehead. Everyone cheered, applauded, and shouted, "Welcome home!" I had trouble keeping my composure. Tears welled up in my eyes as I just stood there as if glued to the floor.

Maria went up to him first, hugging him and greeting him in Spanish as she wiped his face with a tissue and pushed him over to me. Embracing him awkwardly, I couldn't hold back my tears.

"Why are you crying?" he asked. "Aren't you happy to see me?"

"I'm very happy to see you," I answered through my sniffles as Maria gave me another tissue. "These are tears of joy."

Ed came over and put his arm around my shoulder. "You'd better sit down, Megan, or we'll have to make another trip to the hospital."

I did as I was told.

"I make coffee," Maria said and left for the kitchen.

Chris wheeled his chair next to me, and I took his warm hand in mine. "How do you feel?" I asked.

"Okay, but I can't believe I'm this worn out from the short trip up the mountain. I've driven that route hundreds of times."

I looked at him but remained silent, and he continued, "I'd better get back to my routine in the gym, so I can get in shape for next week." He squeezed my hand affectionately. "It feels good to be home."

Maria returned with coffee on a tray for everyone, and then she went back to let Duchess come in to greet Chris too. Duchess was panting and wagging her tail wildly, but Ed soon led her back out again. Duchess was not an inside dog.

Maria had set the table for four in the kitchen, but Ed went home to Elizabeth for lunch and Joe had left with the van driver.

"Do you want to eat with us, Maria?" Chris said in English, for my benefit, I suppose.

"No, thank you. I go home to my family. You two have a nice time together."

So it was just Chris and me. The casserole was good, and I was hungry. In all the excitement I had forgotten to eat breakfast, and it was way past lunchtime. After I had cleaned up, we went into the living room. There was plenty of open space for Chris to wheel himself around, and he was already getting pretty agile in his chair. His arms were still muscular, and later in the gym he was able to hoist himself out of his chair and onto the workout bench.

"You're doing well," I said as I watched him pull himself into position for his arm exercises, while I stepped onto the elliptical for an easy, no-impact run. We reminisced about all that had happened in the seven plus months since we met last summer, and we talked about our son and the future. Well, actually I talked, and he mostly listened.

A physical therapist came every morning to help Chris shower and get dressed before working on his legs to try to prevent the muscles from atrophying. The rest of the time, we managed ourselves. In the afternoon we went for long walks. Since he had little feeling in his legs and wouldn't know whether he was hot or cold, I was careful to place blankets around the lower half of his body.

One afternoon, on our way home, we saw a bald eagle suddenly swooping down from a tall tree near Chris's house, soaring out over the lake. I gasped and just stood there rooted to the ground, staring at it. "What a majestic sight," I exclaimed. "That surely must mean good luck."

"Yes, they are spectacular," he replied. It picked up a plump duck near the resort, and we waited to see if it would return. It didn't, but we saw it several times after that.

We usually went to bed early, and although I had to adjust my tummy, we would snuggle together as we had done before. Everything seemed so normal.

"Touch me," he said suddenly one night, and I immediately knew what he meant, but he could not feel my hand.

"We couldn't have sex now anyway," I said. "The doctor told me a couple of weeks ago to avoid intercourse; and after the birth there will be a lot of bleeding for a while. I guess that's nature's way of saying 'no more kids for now, thank you very much.'"

"I'm determined to get better," he said optimistically. "You know me. I'm stubborn; I always go after what I want, and I usually get it."

"I know," I said and kissed him on his cheek.

We made preparations for the wedding to take place the following Saturday morning. Chris was in a pensive mood during this time but was a great help. It was hard for him to accept his situation, and I tried to encourage him and told him often that I loved him. However, I also wondered if something was weighing on his mind. Had he, for example, conferred with Ed and Joe about a prenuptial agreement, and had Ed and Joe nixed it? Or, could it be the other way around? No. That didn't make sense. I was tempted to bring it up but decided against it. Why bring up something that must have been settled already?

Ed had volunteered to officiate. As a lieutenant sheriff he said he had long ago obtained a license to perform wedding ceremonies, and in his full uniform he looked the epitome of officialdom and formality. I wore the same simple blue dress I wore the first day of school last fall, while Chris had dug out a fine dark-brown sports coat that I hadn't seen before.

"You look nice," I said.

"Thank you. So do you."

"Thank you." I tried to smile encouragingly and gave him a kiss on his forehead before I turned away and looked at Maria, who was bustling about with glasses and bottles of champagne, her shoulders covered by a colorfully embroidered black Mexican shawl.

"Where did you get that beautiful shawl, Maria," I asked.

"Joe gave it to me for Christmas," she replied. No surprise there. I noticed that she had also put her hair up and had even put on some make-up for the occasion. Again I wondered if she and Joe had had a little fling after Ed and Chris's mother died. Maybe she still carried a torch for Joe. She seemed so much part of the family.

Elizabeth sat quietly on the couch looking thin and frail, but she had made it, and Cheryl made sure she was as comfortable as possible. Jonathan, Sandy, Cindy, and Chad tried their best to put on happy faces, while Joe was unusually quiet and seemingly lost in thought. Because of the icy roads, Susie and Ashley didn't make it, so there was no one to play

Mendelssohn's and Wagner's famous Wedding Songs, but there was plenty of champagne waiting.

"Are you sure you want to go through with this?" Chris asked me suddenly.

"Yes, but *you* don't sound too sure," I replied.

He just sighed and looked away.

"Chris, if you don't want to...."

But before I could finish my sentence, Joe broke in. "You better not screw this one up, son," he said sternly.

Chris looked at his father and then at Ed. "Okay, I was just kidding," he said and flashed his charming smile.

"I don't think anyone is amused," Joe continued. "Least of all Megan."

I remained silent and started reminiscing about my first marriage. Robert and I had been married in a small and somewhat awkward ceremony too. Robert's parents were deceased, and my parents couldn't leave the farm at that time. We had just invited a couple of friends that I haven't seen since. To top it off, we both had the flu, and I was so full of medication that I couldn't stand and had to sit down. But we had shared an apartment together for over a year and knew we were right for each other. The marriage had really been a convenience, a practical formality before we moved to Africa.

"James will be the official photographer." Ed announced. "He's taking photography at the high school and has a new camera."

"Thank you, James. What a great idea! I didn't think of recording the event. Now we'll have photos to display on our coffee table." James's face brightened. He had been sitting by his mother's side, but now he left her to test different angles for his photo shoot. "Are you going to publish your pictures in T*he Mountain Gazette*?" I continued teasingly. James looked at his father.

"No, not this time," Ed answered for him. "But Gary will probably put in a notice about the whole affair. A wedding is news up here you know, Megan,"

And so, we were ready to proceed with the ceremony. I stood by Chris's chair in front of the fireplace as we said our "I do's." Maria opened the champagne and poured glasses for everyone, including herself. For me she had a glass of non-alcoholic Martinelli's® apple cider but I had a sip of champagne too. Then all proposed toasts to our happiness and long lives.

Settlers Inn had agreed to cater the wedding lunch, and the caterers arrived with a light salad and chicken breasts in a delicious sauce that they served on individual plates with mixed vegetables. For dessert, they had brought chocolate mousse, and we finished with coffee. Maria had a place at the big dining room table with the rest of us, but she spent most of the time in the kitchen, evidently uncomfortable with these young people taking over *her* kitchen.

"It won't be much of a wedding night," Chris said loud enough for everyone to hear after the meal was over.

"Oh, stop it," I said as we moved over to the couch for more champagne. "We've already had our wedding night, remember?" I patted my tummy before I gave him a kiss on the cheek. The others laughed, but as I looked up, I saw James's face redden.

"And now, James, I'm officially your Aunt Megan; how do you feel about that?"

"It's good," he said softly.

"And soon you'll have a little cousin."

"Is it true it's going to be a boy?" he wanted to know and looked straight at me. He was looking more and more like Chris and Ed.

"Yes, it is. Do you think you can help me take care of him, maybe play with him sometimes, be his big brother?"

"Yeah, that'll be fun." His awkwardness was suddenly gone.

Ed gave him a big hug, and Elizabeth had a big smile on her face as James went and sat down by her.

When it was all over, I called my mother and told her about the baby and how our marriage ceremony had been delayed because of Chris's accident. As usual she obsessed about my doctorate, and I promised I'd work on it this coming year. Mothers can be so tiresome, but she promised to come out soon to meet her new grandson and son-in-law.

In early February, we went for more tests at USC and received some good news. Chris's spine had been cracked but not severed, and it was healing. He might need surgery, but the prognosis for full recovery looked good. According to the orthopedic surgeon, he should be able to walk again, although it might take a year or two.

"What about other functions?" I asked, but he didn't seem to get what I was hinting at.

"She means sex," the nurse behind him said.

"Oh, I didn't get that," he said apologetically. "But, yes, when he can wiggle his toes, everything else should work too."

We called Joe and Ed with the good news as soon as we returned to the car. Then we drove to my house, where we stayed for several days before we drove up to the mountains. On the sunny slopes, between patches of snow, the daffodils were already peeking out of the seemingly barren ground. Spring. What an amazing time!

EPILOGUE

Daffodils and tulips were in full bloom by the time the contractions started, and I was ready to give birth. Chris called Ed as he usually did when we needed help. Ed was a rock and a saint during this time, although he too must have been under tremendous stress with his wife Elizabeth's illness and his son's grief over the possibility of losing his mother. Ed came with sirens blaring.

"Thank you, Ed," I said as he came barging through the door. "But it's not that urgent. The contractions have just started, and I know from my research that it's going to take a few hours."

"Well, you never know," Ed said. "I've had a few emergency births in my time and so have some of my deputies, so hurry. Come on." He steadied me as we walked to his car.

We drove off in the sheriff's car but without the sirens. After he had dropped me off at the hospital, he went back and brought Chris, so he could be present in the delivery room. I wasn't sure that was a good idea, but Chris wanted to be there.

Although painful, the birthing process was smooth and went fast.

"This was easy," the doctor said when it was all over. "You're built to have babies. I'll see you again in a year."

I think I managed a faint smile.

"Congratulations," he said to Chris. Then he removed his shower cap and left.

The little fellow had lots of black hair, weighed 8 lbs. 10 oz. and measured 21 inches. He was a big guy, according to the young nurse, who didn't look that big herself. To me he looked tiny and helpless. The nurse wiped him off and wrapped him in a blanket. When she placed him in Chris's arms, it was Chris's turn to lose his composure.

The next day we named him John Patrick, John after my grandfather, and Patrick after Chris's.

After we came home, and between his workouts in the gym, Chris would sit for up to half an hour just looking at this little bundle of joy, playing with his tiny hands, and ruffling his unruly hair. He loved to watch me nurse him and "help" Maria and me bathe and change him.

And so life went on. Little John Patrick was an easy baby who slept through the night from the very first day. With Maria doing most of the household chores—it was a big house to take care of—and with Ed and also Joe on call, we survived. Joe had come out of his retirement to keep the business going. He too was a consummate salesman, and the company didn't seem to lack invitations to submit bids. Many of the long-time workers stepped up to the plate as well. They didn't want to lose their jobs, of course, but Chris was also known for taking good care of his people, and it paid off because now they, in turn, took care of him.

Cindy often stopped by as did Cheryl. Cindy admitted she was all thumbs when it came to babies, but when Cheryl took charge, she changed diapers and dressed the little one like a pro. She also helped Ed with Elizabeth, her older sister, and we all became good friends during that time. True, there were many obstacles to overcome, but despite hardships, there were many roses among the thorns.

The End

Don't miss out on your next favorite book!

Join the Satin Romance mailing list
www.satinromance.com/mail.html

ABOUT THE AUTHOR

Kari Sayers graduated from California State University, Long Beach, with a BA in English and an MA in linguistics. She went on two tours with her husband to Saudi Arabia, where she first worked as a music teacher at Riyadh International Community School and then as a journalist for an English newspaper over there, writing under censorship. After returning to the States, she taught ESL (English as a Second Language) at various colleges in the Los Angeles area and finally composition and literature at Marymount California University while also freelancing as a theater, concert and opera reviewer for local newspapers and magazines. She has traveled in 70 foreign countries and 40 states in the United States, including Alaska, Hawaii, and Puerto Rico. She has three grown children and three young grandchildren and lives in Los Angeles with her cat.